# FIRE IN THE FLESH

# FIRE IN THE FLESH

JACK SHERIDAN

CUTTING EDGE

ISBN-13: 978-1-962896-72-6

Published by
Cutting Edge Books
PO Box 8212
Calabasas, CA 91372
www.cuttingedgebooks.com

# Dedication

*For Zula McKay with love*

# CHAPTER ONE

Nothing hurried Rita Karnes. No matter how many cars came beetling up into the open area before the drive-in, no matter how many lights flicked on and off, no matter how many angry horn beeps speared for her attention. She moved in her own good time, her legs long and sure, propped securely on the high heels, thighs firm and generous in the tightness of shorts that dimpled with the sway of her buttocks. She waited languorously at the service window until her trays were ready and then crossed the drive-in lot with full assurance, her full-breasted impudence disturbing the minds and loins of the men who, one arm around their girls, watched her make her rounds.

Rita had been a hop a long time. "It ain't a hard job and the tips is good" was her laconic comment. The guys was all right and the car doors kept 'em in their place. Sometimes, she got to thinking, maybe she ought to wear a bra, especially when one of them long-arm guys reached out quick-like and pinched a bruise on one of 'em, but, most times, she kinda read their minds, saw it coming in their eyes.

Now, as she threaded her way between the cars, hardly mindful of the balance of the Coke glass, the sliding dish of hamburger and chips, she frowned to herself. Somehow, behind her, she could sense Harry, sitting inside at the counter, sucking at his coffee, his thick freckled-mottled hands cradling the cup, his pale, watery blue eyes under the thick red brows watching her, narrowed, alert and knowing.

She came before the bumper of the last of the cars and crossed around to the driver's side. From the open window there were the muted sounds of the radio and, for the moment, she couldn't see him half-sprawled behind the steering wheel. As she fixed the tray to the sill he came sitting up, framed suddenly in the car window, his dark eyes sparkling in the reflection of the neon sign, his teeth bursting white in the weathered tan of his country face.

"Thought you was never comin'." He grinned.

She sniffed, fastening the last of the clamps. "You ain't the only hot shot on the lot, boy."

"Them other bastards don't matter," he dismissed easily.

She had taken the order pad from the pocket of her blouse and was marking down the charge. Troy Bannock let his lids drop slightly and his gaze rested on the thrust of her nipple against the sheen of the thin blouse. Unconsciously he moistened his lips and shifted on the seat.

She looked up suddenly. "How come you ain't got a date?"

His gaze broke and he glanced at her with a faint flush. "She's gone to Dallas with her folks."

"Lone wolfin', huh?"

"Might could put it that way, I reckon."

Rita's eyes veiled slightly. From where she stood on the car's side she could just make out the long legs, shadowed from the light that caught the dull brightness of the rivets on his levis, could see the flicking glint of the sign's glare on the bunched blond hairs that cropped in the hollow of his throat. "Big good-lookin' character like you ought not to have much trouble pickin' somethin' up," she observed dryly.

"That's what I been thinkin'," he said quietly, his eyes hungry on her.

Rita felt that something somewhere inside her give a turn, felt as she always did whenever Troy Bannock came hunkering around. "I'm a workin' girl," she sniffed.

"You ain't always workin'," he grunted.

"When I ain't workin', my time's taken up," she said. "You're forgettin'."

"I ain't forgettin'," he murmured wearily. His thick lashes played against his cheeks for a second. Then his eyes wide, looking into hers, she saw the touch of challenge come into them. "No more'n you're forgettin' sometimes."

Tardily she moved back, avoided the swift, reaching fingers that darted through the car window.

"Cut it!" she hissed. She tossed her head once sharply, her reddish hair kicking back from her shoulders. "We got company."

Troy scowled and his glance found the glassed front of the building. "Him?"

"It's his night off," she said. "He's been sittin' there all night, drinkin' coffee, watchin' me."

"Ain't he got nothin' better to do on a day off?"

Her smile was thin. "He gets ideas maybe I ain't toein' the line like I ought."

Troy's eyes came back to her. "Don't know where he could get them ideas."

"He's got imagination," she giggled. "A whopper." She backed away and restored the pad to the mounded pocket and pressed out the wrinkling shorts over flaring hips. "I gotta get at it."

Troy made no move to reach for the hamburger and Coke. He still watched her cagily. Again he wet his lips. "Tomorrow night?"

"Ain't your girl friend comin' back?"

"Not 'til Monday."

Rita's voice was thin and she shifted her glance to the vacancy over the car roof. "When you're goin' with one girl, you oughtn't to be playin' around so much," she pronounced.

"Balls!" Troy reached for the hamburger without taking his eyes from her. He spoke with his mouth full. "It ain't the same thing."

"Yeah." She found his face and there was a fleeting shadow in her eyes. "Yeah, I guess I found that out a long time ago."

She turned and went back toward the lights. Troy sat watching her, the hamburger arrested. After a moment, when she had been blocked from view by the cars in front, he reached down with his free hand and jerked the levis down a little. Seemed like every time they got washed they were just that much tighter.

Sitting as he was, hunched forward on the counter, the big fleshy hands cupping the coffee, the diamond ring sharply glinting in its bed of reddish short hairs on his finger, his head turned slightly, his little blue eyes cold and intent on the semidarkness of the lot, Harry Marvel looked like a malevolent tortoise. He wore slacks and a fresh T-shirt and the red hair furled along the neckline, bunching in a hedgerow along the back of his shoulders. His forearms were thick and hairy, specked with the tannish orange spots that the sun brought out, and above the elbow, his thick biceps pushed hard against the stretching short sleeve of the shirt.

Harry Marvel's hair had thinned as he had wallowed into his thirties and now there were only the long strands trying to do the work over the perpetual shine of his sweaty scalp.

Most people around town caught themselves looking at his lips as he spoke or when he sat quiet. They were thick lips, full and sensual, with a faint drawing of something undefinably wicked and cruel, something intangible. They never lost this identifying characteristic, even in the moments of rare surface laughter. Somehow, the evil always remained.

As Rita came across the narrow unoccupied strip facing the front door of the diner, crossing to the service window, Harry Marvel's lips tightened. His eyes seemed to shrink a little more within the fleshy folds of his face. He tightened his grip on the cup and, suddenly, he took his hands from the cup before he crushed it.

He put the butts of both hands against the rounded counter edge and shoved back, sliding his thick hams from the stool, and pulled himself to full height. His body seemed to swell, the sharp outlines of his pectoral muscles edged vividly on the thin white shirt, hard and sculptured. He hitched his slacks in place, moving his belt clasp a notch as he moved smoothly toward the double glass doors that opened on the parking lot.

Rita was waiting by the service window for her order. She slumped a little, letting the harsh edge of the windowsill cut into the soft side above the hip bone, letting the wooden lip carry her tired weight. Her only recognition when Harry Marvel came out into the open was to raise her head slightly and purse her mouth irritably. The weariness came welling up through her until it seemed as if she were sinking down into some kind of void. Harry had that mean look, like he was going to start something again. The little bitter taste came to her mouth. She sure as hell couldn't take any more tonight!

"Who's the guy you was battin' the breeze with out there?" he said quietly, his eyes intent.

"What guy you talkin' about?" She met his little eyes coolly.

"You know goddam well what guy I'm talkin' about." Harry nodded sharply. "That joker out behind the cars."

"Oh, him." There was a scuffing as the order slid across the sill and Rita straightened and turned her back on him, setting things in order on the tray. "Just one of the kids," she offered airily.

"For a kid he's got goddam big hands," Harry grunted.

She turned around with the tray held in both hands. Her eyes were wide and hot on him. They were almost the same height, he and she, and she met his look coolly, levelly. "You know, Harry," she said slowly. "There's times you let that sonofabitchin' thinkin' of yours get 'way out of line."

"It's not my thinkin' gettin' out of line," he said. "It ain't got nothin' to do with thinkin'. I don't go for nothin' that's mine gettin' out of line."

"Yeah?" Rita baited sardonically.

"Yeah." His big hand came up and his fingers caught her arm, dug into the flesh, holding her fast. "I see some bastard playin' with you and somebody's gonna get busted one good, see?"

"Oh, for God's sake, Harry, if I didn't know you better, I'd think you was drunk!"

His grip tightened. "I'm watchin', kid, don't you forget it. I got my eye on you."

She gave a violent lurch, pulling herself from his clutch. "Goddamit, Harry, lemme go! I got customers! You keep hangin' 'round here makin' an ass of yourself and you're gonna get me fired, hear? Whyn't you go home, go see a show, go somewheres ...?" She half turned and flung her words at him. "Go get drunk once in a while like any other man. I'd a helluva lot rather know you was drunked up than this way, actin' like we was married or somethin'."

She went out across the shadowed lot, the tray now balanced with professional ease in one hand, her pace quickening, the high heels tapping an angry staccato on the pavement.

Harry Marvel clamped his teeth hard, following her progress with smoky eyes. There was a faint pulsing in the reddish jowls, and his hands were rolled up into heavy fist-balls at his sides. He watched until he had lost sight of her and then slowly the tension began to lessen.

Martha Devine watched him from across the steamy kitchen. She wished he wouldn't come hanging around the place while Rita was working. Rita was one of the best, but whenever her boy friend Harry Marvel showed up like this, she went all nervous, made mistakes, slowed down filling orders. Martha crossed the hot room and rested her elbows on the inside sill.

"Look, Harry," she began quietly, "whyn't you be a good boy and run along, huh? Rita's got her hands full tonight, it bein' Saturday and all."

"It ain't Rita's hands bein' full I'm worryin' about," he sneered.

"My god, Harry, busy as she is, how's she gonna get time to horse around? Use your head, man."

Harry eyed the neat woman before him distrustfully. "There's always time for horsin' around," he grunted.

"Not in no drive-in on a Saturday, son," Martha remarked dryly.

"If I ever catch ..." he began, the flame breaking out in his eyes again.

"This ain't no fishin' ground, Harry. You best get on home or somewheres."

Harry opened his mouth to retort. The eyes appraising him behind the screen of glasses cooled his anger. He made a half motion with his open hands and turned and glanced out over the ranks of parked cars. She wasn't anywhere to be seen, she could be back there getting herself all loved up, for all he knew. He straightened and sucked down his breath.

Martha Devine watched him as he went along the side of the building and threaded his way between the parked cars until he came out under the bright light of the street lamp on the corner. She saw him hesitate, glance back over the block of cars and then slowly cross the intersection and start down the sidewalk on the next block.

He's probably heading for the rink, she thought. Harry Marvel had only two things in his life, the skating rink and Rita. The rink was a howling success; Rita—Martha shrugged. Now, Rita was a different proposition as far as Harry Marvel was concerned. Troubled, she turned from the window and walked slowly to the kitchen.

Rita said nothing when she came to get the empty tray from Troy's car. Her face was troubled in the shadows and her eyes, as they met his, were dark.

"Be seein' you tomorrow?"

His question only brought a deepening in the cleft between her brows. There was a faint, imperceptible shrug of her shoulders and then she turned and picked her way down the passage between the cars ahead.

Troy Bannock sat for a moment staring at the place where she had gone from view. Ever since he'd come out of the movie there'd been that banding across his chest, that fierce, demanding urge of his loins. He'd kinda counted on getting Rita off somewhere after she'd finished her shift, maybe. Now, in his mind's eye he could see the fullness of her bared breasts, taste the ridging points of her nipples, feel the quick breathless opening of her body, know at last the tight lock of her legs, the driving, sweating thrust of himself and the spending wash of the moment of explosive fulfillment.

With an effort Troy forced down the hungering. He straightened, slid over under the wheel and started the car. As he carefully backed out into the street, his eyes swept the lot for a last look at her but she was nowhere to be seen. There wasn't nothing else to do but head for home, he reckoned.

# CHAPTER TWO

Outside the biting wind of the norther came gusting over the naked fields, ignoring the spikes of last year's cotton, racing viciously toward the old weather-beaten buildings that huddled forlornly against the flat slate-gray of the late March sky. Gone was the tempered warmth of the premature spring day that was yesterday. The bitter wind worked rudely along the scuffed boards of the old house, seeking out the cracks and splits, eating avidly into the resisting frame.

In his room Troy Bannock bent forward and stared at himself in the dresser mirror. He turned his head slightly from side to side, examining his cheeks closely, making sure. With a grimace he eyed the strong, straight line of his teeth. He'd always been damned glad he hadn't gotten that rutted brown erosion of West Texas in the enamel like so many of the other guys.

The faint, thin, stinging lash of the cold wind curled around his bared shoulders. He stepped back, straightening with a scowl. He glanced across at the ill-fitting window, through which the wind whispered, saw the fitful stir of the cheap, plain curtain. Even the open gas heater at his feet couldn't keep the place warm enough.

Twisting he snagged the jockey shorts from the bed behind him and drew them up his long, glint-haired legs, snapping the elastic band with a crack against his hard young flesh, tight against the narrowness of his hips. Standing now, legs spraddled, Troy eyed himself with deep satisfaction.

From the top of his blond, short-spiked crew cut to the large heavy feet, he was a man, even if he had to say so himself. Slowly, thoughtfully, he brought his big hand up to the base of his throat, to where the hairs curled in the little pocket there, and spread his fingers, his palm flat against the soft blond mass of his upper chest.

Troy often did this in the privacy of the little room. He'd just stand there looking at himself, eyeing himself as if he were someone else entirely, someone quite different from himself, judging what he saw as he might some other guy in a school gym or down at the lakes or at some pool. He'd bring his hand down slowly, just as he was doing now, in a kind of circling motion, so that the hot palm would pass over the small, hard points of his nipples, down to the good, hard flat of his belly.

His fingers strayed a moment below. He hefted the bulge of his manhood, proud always that he had so much, cocky that even though he was the younger—five years younger than his brother—he was bigger in every respect, even there.

Troy Bannock's chin lifted slightly and he smiled faintly. He was big, he was strong and he had him a girl who knew it. One thing for damn sure, Nancy Collins was gonna have herself a man.

"You gawkin' at yourself again, for cryin' out loud?"

Troy's eyes flickered slightly and he scowled at the image of his sister-in-law. She was draped against the nicked door jamb, picking at her teeth idly with a shriveled stalk, watching him with a faint curl of derision tugging at her full, sensual features.

"Whyn't you mind your own goddam business, stay the hell outta my room!" Troy yelled.

"I ain't in your room, honey," Cressy Bannock barbed. " 'Pears like I'm outside here in the hall, just passin' by. Gosh, I might as well stop and have me a look too, since it's on exhibition again!"

Troy smirked. "Ain't often I reckon you get a look at a real man."

"Could be," Cressy agreed smoothly. Her eyes moved carefully, unguardedly over the stretch of his body and caught momentarily at his waist. "There's sure a helluva lot of you, boy, if you know what I mean."

"Funny, I was just thinkin' that myself." Troy grinned.

Cressy Bannock brought her eyes up to her young brother-in-law's face. She took the stalk from her mouth and wet her lips carefully. "Way I see it, Troy," she said, "it ain't what you got, so much as it's what you do with it."

"I ain't had me no complaints." He had turned back to the mirror.

There was a little silence, broken only by the eddying whisper of the March wind. Troy stepped over to the lone chair and caught up his good slacks.

"You mean your girl friend Nancy?" she ventured.

Troy threw a sharp glance at her. "I didn't say nothin' like that."

"Sometimes I get the idea maybe she's too good for you, that one," Cressy said.

The swift, sharp anger spumed inside Troy. He flung the slacks on the bed, stepped quickly across the room. Cressy made no move to step aside, to abandon her post by the door frame. Her gray-green eyes glinted as she raised her head and stared up into Troy's tight young face.

"I want you should stay the hell outta my room, hear?" He grabbed fumblingly at her and shoved hard, pushing her back into the shadows of the hall.

The crash of the slamming door rocked the frame house. From somewhere behind the thin panel there came the sound of an echoing laugh as the woman went on to the front of the house.

Goddam nosy bitch, he raged, always stickin' her snout in things don't concern her! Always lookin', always sneakin' up without warnin', just standin' around, lickin' her lips, keepin' her eyes on things that were none of her business!

Angrily, hastily Troy dragged on the slacks, yanked the zipper in place. Muttering to himself he fought his way into the T-shirt and stuffed the end unevenly inside the trousers. Grunting he sat on the edge of the bed and grabbed his socks and shoes, working feverishly with them.

As his hand went to the brown porcelain knob of the closed door he paused. The vagrant thought went through his mind like a stray bit of paper tumbled across the hard land outside. "Maybe she's too good for you, that one." That's what Cressy had said. Maybe she was. No matter how hard he tried, she wouldn't let him get near, never let him fool around like the others did. Every time he reached out to find the hard-apple thrust of her small breasts, she managed to brake him.

His eyes flashed hotly at the remembered, taunting form of his sister-in-law leaning against the door jamb. Just you gimme time, he promised grimly, I'll get there, you wait and see.

Troy opened the door quietly. From the front of the house there was the murmur of talk from her and the folks. He turned and went swiftly down the short hall, through the kitchen and out the back door.

Far off in the field he caught sight of the moving black king-pin silhouette that was his brother. That was Tom, out walking the rim of the section, no matter if the wind was choppin' hunks out of flesh with icy blades. Tom was kinda slow and stupid, kinda like the old man, sweatin' one minute, freezin' his balls off the next, tryin' to coax enough to live on off a few sections of land that fought back all the time. That's all Tom had now, would ever have, the land and a crack at Cressy every now and then to keep his temper down.

Troy crossed the yard and slid behind the wheel of the reconverted 52 Ford. He'd done a lot of work on this baby, souped her up plenty, weighted the body, cut out all the fancy stuff, sleeked her down right. His eyes found Tom once more as he pressed the starter. The roar from the engine came bursting into the clearing between the house and barn and he saw Tom's head lift and a hand raise.

"Screw you, Jack!" he muttered. He yanked the steering wheel and the car skidded crazily on the frozen pan of the earth. With a faint yelp from the tires, the car shot forward and tore off down the short tracked lane that led to the paved road and town.

Inside the house Cressy and her in-laws paused in what they had been saying. As one their eyes went to the curtained window and they watched the low-slung car go careening along the road, turning on the highway, heading south, disappearing in a matter of seconds.

Ma Bannock cleared her throat and brushed absently at a wisp of gray hair that fretted on her brow. "He's a good boy," she murmured defensively, as if someone had ventured an opinion otherwise. Cressy's eyes gave her nothing and she glanced apprehensively at her husband. "He's real bright," she added lamely, tardily.

Will Bannock said nothing. His arthritic fingers found an opening in his khaki shirt and he thoughtfully rubbed against the wiry graying hairs on his chest.

"He sure don't look or act nothin' like Tom," Cressy commented with a trace of acid. "You'd sure never know they was brothers, believe you me!"

"Like or not, they are," Will said suddenly. He let his eyes stray to the colorless outdoors and sat musing for a moment or two. "Sometimes, when I'm sittin' alone, I get to thinkin' about the boys," he said slowly. "Seems right hard to realize Tom's almost twenty-four, that Troy's a nineteen-year-old now, a man."

"Man? Seems to me he acts more like a damn fool kid most times instead of a man. Tom's the man!"

Ma smiled cautiously. "That's 'cause Tom's your man, Cressy. It's what you should think."

Cressy's eyes widened slightly; she looked at her mother-in-law silently for a moment. "Yeah ..." she agreed absently. "Yeah, Ma, guess you're right."

"When Troy and Nancy are married and settled down proper, that's the way she'll be feelin' about him," Ma stated complacently.

"Just when are they gonna get married, you know?" Cressy asked,

Will Bannock stirred uneasily in his chair and shifted his cane to the other side.

"You hurtin' again, Will?" Ma moved as if she were going to him.

Will waved his hand, stopped her. "Ain't nothin', just the old crimp again." He grunted and hoisted his twisted body a little higher in the chair. "Goddam bein' like this!" he exploded.

"Will, please ... don't go to swearin'."

Will's eyes lighted with a grim fire. "Ain't swearin'," he grunted. "That's my prayer for today. Every day I damn the day I lost my health and God hears it and knows how I'm feelin' about it. I ain't about to let Him forget it!"

"That's blasphemin'," Ma said sadly.

"It ain't," Pa protested quietly. "It's just lettin' Him know, is all."

"You heard when Troy's thinkin' of gettin' married?" Cressy persisted.

"They ain't even got engaged yet," Will snorted. "Won't be for a good spell yet. Not 'til after Troy's got his schoolin' done."

Cressy stared at her father-in-law. "You mean, at his age, Troy's really thinkin' about goin' back to school like he talks about, goin' off to the University at Austin?"

"That's right."

"Well, of all the foolishness ..."

Will Bannock fixed his daughter-in-law with a calm eye. He wet his lips and folded his hands loosely in his lap. "I reckon I'd like to see him stay on the place, work the land. Only when you got brains to use like Troy's got, Cressy, it don't matter how old he is, if'n it's what he wants to do. Tom, he likes the land, that's his life. Troy, I wish he did, too ... only he don't like the land, he says. He don't want that kind of life. Troy wants somethin' else and he's got his eye fixed on it. To get what he says he wants he's gotta have more schoolin', I reckon, the University. So, he's been workin', savin' up these last three years and come next fall he'll go to the school, he says. He's got him a plan."

"What about Nancy, what about them?"

"They'll be gettin' married one of these here days, if that's what's right for 'em," Ma said securely. "Maybe before Troy goes off to that Austin school."

"He said so?" Cressy demanded.

"Not in so many words, Troy ain't said nothin'." Ma smiled. "Troy ain't no talker about himself, he's a doer, like Pa. But ... you wait and see. I'm right."

# CHAPTER THREE

Nancy Collins sat clear over on her side of the car seat, her right shoulder jammed tight against the door, sitting so that her body faced Troy on an angle. Curiously she studied his face as he guided the car down the center of the broad street.

He sat hunched forward, his big hands gripping the upper portion of the steering wheel, his gaze intent on the sweep of the road ahead. Nancy kept watching him, seeing the play of color on his lean jaw as they passed the reds, yellows and greens of the stop lights and the neon signs of the downtown district.

The girl said nothing. She knew he was angry with her, annoyed because she had made him stop pawing her during the movie. The minute they got alone it was always like that, Troy's hands seemed to multiply somehow. They caught at her shoulders and went sliding down over her blouse and now and then came to her thighs and worked their way insistently, relentlessly.

Nancy sighed and absently brushed back her brown hair from her forehead. She folded her hands again and looked at them with troubled eyes. It wasn't as if she didn't want him to touch her. She had a feeling every so often that he knew that, too; that's why he tried and kept on trying.

And there were times, even if she had to admit it privately to herself, when something funny began happening inside her, when everything in her turned into a kind of melting, when she felt as if her insides were opening up like the petals of a budding plant. Once or twice, maybe more than that, there had been that wild desire, the wanting to let him touch her. But she couldn't, she knew that. Other girls did it all the time; they did it in parked cars along the roads around the lakes, out on the country farm roads, parked at drive-in movies, like tonight.

Nancy Collins couldn't explain why, she just knew she couldn't have it that way, that sneaking, well ... dirty, kind of way. Somehow she wasn't ready for the other yet. So, she kept his hands off her as much as she could, even though she could have cried out at times to have him touch her.

Everything was safer that way, safer and righter. Later on, well, after they got married ... if they did ... every-thing would be as it should be. Only not now, not yet.

Without saying a word Troy headed for the cluster of gleaming cars pulled up at the White Owl Drive-in. Carefully he edged the car between two larger convertible jobs and cut the engine. With scarcely a glance in her direction, he cleared his throat.

"What'll you have?"

"The usual." Her voice was very small. She eyed him worriedly for a moment, then straightened and glanced over the lot. "Nobody's here yet. It's too early, I guess."

"Everybody don't have to go home in the middle of the evenin'!" Troy snorted.

Nancy glanced at him, opened her mouth to try to point out again that after the long drive up from Dallas that day, her folks wanted to get to bed early, that they'd stay up until she got in safely, and she couldn't help it. She said nothing. When Troy got like this, that lower lip pushed out in full fight, there wasn't any use in saying anything.

Suddenly Rita was at the window, her eyes wide, her lips full, her attention solely on Troy. Nancy's lips tightened as the car hop's long fingers with their dark-red nails reached in and tweaked the curling hairs along the top of the T-shirt.

"What're you kids gonna have?"

"Same as usual." Troy's eyes had narrowed as he stared up into her face.

Rita gave the hairs a final pluck and with a laugh withdrew her hand. At no time had she looked across to where Nancy sat. She straightened and took the pad from the blouse pocket. "Cheeseburgers and Cokes, right?"

"Right."

Troy's eyes remained on the retreating figure. He wet his lips and unconsciously rubbed his palms on his flank.

Nancy's cheeks burned and she turned her head, trying to keep her eyes busy elsewhere, peering into the half-shadowed recesses of the parked cars. She could feel the warmth of him near her and finally she had to look back.

"You're still going back to school in the fall, aren't you, Troy?" she asked.

"Maybe."

"I hope so," she said primly, smoothing down her skirt. "You've got a good brain and you've been working so long to save the money and all. You can't change your mind; there's no reason to!"

"I get by."

"That isn't enough!"

"Sometimes I wonder."

"Troy, sometimes I don't understand you, really I don't."

"Lots of times you don't understand me." His glance was brief but meaningful.

Nancy flushed. She picked nervously at the hem of her skirt. "I'm sorry, Troy, really I am...."

Troy sucked in a deep draught from his cigarette and let the smoke trickle slowly through his nostrils. "Forget it. Maybe I was gettin' too eager."

They said nothing as Rita came with the tray. Expertly she fastened it to the side and took Troy's money. As she made the change, her fingers seemed to trail lightly across the ball of his thumb and her eyes narrowed slightly.

"You come back, you hear?" she said softly.

Nancy took her eyes from the scene at the window and tried to swallow the first bite. Maybe she had misunderstood; maybe she was reading too much into the casual, everyday words. Maybe she was just looking for things.

"Nice kid," Troy offered blandly, his eyes on the undulating hips making their way back to the service window.

"She's not much of a kid!" Nancy retorted bitterly. "Why, she must be twenty-five or more!"

"She don't act so old," Troy remarked knowingly.

Talk like this made Nancy nervous, unsure. She knew all about car hops and what they did nights after they got off work. Ellen Thompson had been a car hop and before she got finished she'd had a baby and a peck of trouble besides.

They finished their burgers in silence and drank the last of the Cokes. In a little while Rita came and silently removed the tray. She paid only the briefest attention to Troy, a faint gleam in her eyes as she turned away.

"Let's go now, Troy?" Nancy broke his attention on the retreating hop.

"Oh, Christ, all right!" he exploded. He automatically switched on the key, stamped on the starter and shoved the gear in reverse. The car thrust back abruptly, narrowly missing the neighboring cars, and shot out across the broad street. With screaming tires it leaned heavily on the turn and straightened its course nearly a block from the drive-in.

In front of the Collins house Troy cut the engine and the stillness of the dark, deserted, residential street came flooding in on them, holding them silent under a kind of thick weight. Troy sat hunched forward, his eyes set on the void ahead, his lips thin, drawn against his teeth.

Nancy stirred and moved her feet. Her eyes flicked over Troy and she wet her lips. "I'm sorry, Troy, really I am." She sighed helplessly. "Nothing went right tonight, did it?"

"It's all right. Forget it."

He looked suddenly like a little boy to her, his lips pushed out like that in a sulky pout, his eyes muddied. She reached out and found his upper arm.

"Troy?"

He gave no indication he heard.

"Troy?"

The fingers slid up under the short sleeve of the T-shirt and pressed lightly against the hard bulge of his biceps. "I am sorry … truly."

Troy closed his eyes. Then he turned slowly. He studied her curiously for a moment. Then his hands took her shoulders. He drew her close to him. "It's just I'm so goddam crazy about you, honey, I can't think of nothin' else but you and how damn much I want you, how I need you." He spoke against the smooth, cool slope of her neck and she shivered slightly as his hot breath played along her flesh.

"I know." Her fingers stroked the smooth hard flesh. She pulled him closer, despite all the warning feelings. "I know, honey, I know.…

Nancy was conscious and in complete control. For a moment there was the memory of the ripe, melon buttocks of the woman Rita in her mind and her grasp on Troy tightened. She felt his hand come feeling along the curve of her breasts and felt his fingers alive on the fabric of her blouse. She knew she ought to stop him now but she did nothing. Her breath snagged and began to pulse as he stroked along the thin material with his thumb. For a moment she had that wild desire to lie back against the seat, to tear at her clothes, fling them from her, to lay herself open for him, to feel his hands, his mouth upon her body, to give, to yield, to let the fires come sweeping fiercely through every fiber of her being.

The sudden, shocking touch of him between her thighs blasted the fantasy. With a surge of power she struggled back against the car door and shoved at his shoulders.

"No, no ... Troy, please ... no!"

She slipped away, taking herself from his seeking hands. She found the door handle and wrenched down as hard as she could. The door swung heavily and the cold air came bursting into the car shockingly. Nancy caught herself before she toppled out on the dead grass of the parking strip. She went sliding forward, her feet finding the solid ground away from the side of the car. She stood, one hand against her lips, sucking her breath down inside her, cold, deep, steadying.

Troy was half-sprawled across the seat, hands outstretched, fingers crooked from the attempt to grab her before she escaped. Now he fought to bring his body straight behind the wheel.

She backed away a step, shook her head as the lock of his door clicked.

"No, Troy ... it's all right. I'll go on in alone. You don't have to bother."

As she spoke, the front porch light flashed on, the screen door pushed open slightly. Herbert Collins stood waiting for his daughter, squinting through the sharp brightness of the porch light.

Nancy turned and ran swiftly across the lawn to the steps of the house. Turning she waved back to the car. "Good night, Troy," she called. "I ... it was nice, thanks." Her voice carried the note of worried uncertainty.

There was no indication in Troy's voice of anything out of the way as he leaned across the seat and waved through the open car window. "See you Saturday?"

Nancy's head turned and her eyes rose to meet her father's smiling gaze. He had not come forward, had said nothing. All he was doing was simply waiting for her to come inside so he could lock up and they could all get to bed. She turned.

"Sure, Troy ..." she called. "Sure, if you want."

Even parked here in the protection of the ghostly, silvered pile of the abandoned old gin, they couldn't escape the jabbing darts of the wintry blasts which came sneaking in, filtering through the false insulation of doors and windows and floor boards. It seemed as if the coldest part of any day was around two o'clock in the morning.

Troy Bannock settled himself back, wedged in where the car door met the stiff, plastic seat cover. His long legs stretched out across the seat, spread, with his left leg almost on the floor boards, making room for her slim, long-legged body between. Leaning back against his chest, she was still now and her hair fuzzed against his nose and snagged on his beard stubble.

Rita shivered and brought Troy's free hand to her belly. She worked the tips of his big fingers down inside the tight band of the snug shorts and giggled faintly. In her other hand she held the half-pint bottle; now she brought it to her lips and took a sip. Then she raised it aloft so he could see and heard him chuckle as he took it and killed what was left.

Rita sighed, snuggled down and closed her eyes. "I'm sure glad you came back, like you said you would. When I seen her come back from Dallas early, I figured you wouldn't. I sure am glad."

Troy twisted; he rolled down the window a bit and dropped the empty bottle on the ground outside. He quickly ran up the window against the cold air blast. His arm loosened; his fingers came around to catch at her unfettered breast. "Me, too," he muttered thickly.

They were silent. In the backwash of their tempestuous lovemaking there was now only a sated kind of peace, weariness.

Rita worked herself to a sitting position. She shoved his long legs off the seat. "You know somethin', I gotta get goin', sonny. God knows, I don't want no more trouble when I get home."

Troy's hands came out of the gloom to find her shoulders but she shook him off easily.

"Uh-uh," she laughed throatily. "You just don't never get enough. Maybe you ought to go into the stud business or somethin', right around the clock."

Troy moistened his lips. He watched her straighten her clothes, fasten the buttons of the blouse again. He made no attempt to straighten, to start the car; he just lolled back and watched.

At length Rita glanced across at him, motioned vaguely toward the dashboard. "Well, sonny boy, you had it. Let's get goin'."

Troy grunted and his fingers found the key. As the car headed back toward the distant smear of lights against the sky that was the town, Rita sat back smoking silently, watching him as he drove.

"Tell me somethin'," she began finally, raising her voice against the rush of the wind outside and the roar of the souped-up engine.

"Yeah?"

"You and that cute little girl you go 'round with, the one tonight."

A faint frown shadowed on Troy's face. He kept his eyes on the road. "Yeah ... what about her?"

"You plannin' on somethin' serious there, maybe?"

"Maybe."

Rita nibbled the edge of her lip and glanced out into the black, solid night. Not looking back at him, she drew a deep breath and said her piece. "She's a nice clean kid. You want to go easy there, boy, none of the rough stuff, not like with us, with you and me."

Troy's eyes flashed as he glanced at her half-turned back. "It ain't the same."

"Yeah." Rita picked a bit of tobacco from her lip and examined it carefully on the tip of her finger. "Like you say, it ain't the same." She murmured, "I reckon you're right."

A block from the drive-in she reached out and touched his forearm. "Best let me off here."

"Why ... it ain't out of my way, runnin' you downtown."

A quick flare of irritation burst on Rita's face. "Here, I said. Stop this goddam hot-rod and lemme off here." Her eyes had narrowed; her gaze was up ahead, fixed on the clump of cars bunched in front of the all-night restaurant.

"Okay, okay," Troy grunted. "If that's what you want."

"That's what I want." She fumbled with the door as the car stopped, shoved it open and got out.

Before she could slam the door, he had leaned over and blocked its closing with his fingers. "See you again ... sometime?"

Rita stood back, away from the car, her hair fired in the halo of the street light. She eyed him speculatively, her head cocked slightly. She had no right running around with him at all, not with Harry cremating himself every night being jealous and all and this here nothing but a kid. She stiffened and moved back toward the sidewalk under the spidery shadow of a leafless maple. Fooling around like this was a good way to get in a pack of trouble and hurting trouble, at that!

Only, as she glanced back at the car, saw the blond brightness of his head as he waited for his answer, she wet her lips. There was a helluva lot of man there, kid or no kid! He had a lot of what made things kinda worth while out of all this mess. What he was packing around was just right for what she needed.

"Yeah, sure, kid ..." She nodded and her voice suddenly thickened. "We'll be gettin' together ... see you around ... sometime."

# CHAPTER FOUR

The gray light of morning filtered into the kitchen, lighting but not bringing any warmth to the old house. Ma Bannock stood lumped in front of the stove, returning the stare of the egg yolks in the pan before her. At the table behind her, Will Bannock scratched his stubbled jaw and peered curiously out the window overlooking the fields.

"Don't look like it's warmin' up much," he commented sourly.

"March's an empty kind of month, I always think," Ma said. "It's empty and dead, sort of. There's times I don't reckon I like March."

Will's nails scraped against his beard in the quiet of the room. "Times like this I reckon I'm sort of glad we got rid of the stock, Ma. That gettin' out before day come was kinda hard this time of year, remember?"

"We ain't had no complaints since," Ma agreed quietly. " 'Cept now for the drought." There was a slightly puzzled, hurt quality in her tone, as if she might be considering that the trouble was purposely set before the Bannocks alone, that God Himself was testing the Bannock strength all over again. "Sure hope there's gonna be a change this year. Tom was sayin' things just got to change."

Will hunched forward and laid his thick arms on the table top. He opened and closed his big gnarled hands pain-fully. "Was sayin' on the radio last night the president's comin' down himself to see what can be done."

Ma flipped the eggs carefully before she turned and looked down on the thinning gray hairs of her husband's bowed head. "Land sakes, what good's that gonna do, Will, comin' down to have a look? You gotta live with it; you can't just look at it. He can't make no rain, can he?"

Will scowled and clasped his thickening fingers tight. "Must be somethin' somebody can do, Ma. He wouldn't be flyin' down here lookin' 'round if there wasn't. I reckon a big man like that knows what he's doin'."

Ma's lips thinned faintly and her eyes lifted, narrowing at the sight of the angry land outside. "Maybe ..." she murmured. "Only, spendin' all that money just to go lookin' at nothin' ... throwin' good money after bad, if you was to ask me."

The sound of Cressy's steps in the narrow short hall caught Ma's attention. The daughter-in-law stood in the doorway, her fingers groping with the last button on the fly of her tight, clean levis. "Mornin'," she greeted brightly.

Ma eyed Cressy disapprovingly. "Rightly 'pears you'd finish buttonin' your clothes in your room, Cressy," she rebuked.

Cressy laughed, tossing the mop of hair away from her shoulders. "Aw, Ma, you can't see nothin'. It ain't like as if Pa here was to come out all open." She laughed against the flush of the older woman's face. "Now, that might be somethin' to see!" She crossed over swiftly and leaned down to kiss the top of Will's head. He smiled and reached up, patting the fleshy part of her arm affectionately.

"Nonetheless, folks does what they has to do in the proper places," Ma persisted.

"Oh, come off it, Ma...." Cressy stepped over to the stove and sniffed at the pots and pans. "Anything I can help with?"

"Everything's done now," Ma announced. "I reckon as how I'm kinda used to doin' for myself in my own kitchen."

Cressy grinned. Her arm encircled Ma's thick waist and she squeezed lightly. "I'm real sorry I was late gettin' up this mornin', Ma." She took the plate of hot bread and crossed to the table, setting it in front of Will. Turning back she glanced at Ma and grinned. "Truth is that handsome son of yours, Ma, the way he wants to go foolin' around mornin's is just plain sinful."

Ma's lids flickered and she glanced away in embarrassment. She'd never in a million years get used to the out-spoken ways of young people today.

"What's so sinful?"

Tom Bannock came into the kitchen and paused, his eyes bright and alive, passing from his mother's flushed face to that of his wife, then down to his father before they came to linger again on his wife's full parted lips.

"You ought to know!" Cressy giggled. "You best sit down right now. You and me just wound up in the dog house."

"What, with Ma?" Tom grabbed at his mother as she tried to pass to the table. He fondled the back of her neck with his rough fingers and laughed as she angrily squirmed away.

"You know good and well I don't like no foolin' around in the kitchen mornin's, Tom Bannock," she scolded.

The four of them bent their heads over the table as Will returned the thanks. Then the business of eating began. No one had mentioned the empty chair at the table; no one had spoken Troy's name. Yet each of them noticed.

"Mornin'."

Four pairs of eyes rose from the concentration on food and came to the boy in the doorway. Troy stood shoving the ends of the T-shirt down inside the tight waistband of an old, faded pair of levis. His eyes were puffed and he grinned sheepishly as he came on into the room.

"You missed the thanks," Ma accused.

Troy flushed. "I reckon I just had a hard time gettin' awake this mornin'."

"You ought, comin' in the time you did," Will remarked dryly. "Where was you all night?"

Troy dropped heavily into the empty chair and hunched up to the table. He kept his face averted from his father's inquisitive eyes and reached out across the table for the egg platter. "Oh, just around." He shrugged.

"Just around," his father echoed.

"Around ... like where?" Tom asked suddenly.

Troy's eyes rose to his brother's face and he scowled. "Just around, like I said."

Cressy glanced sidelong at her husband and then at Troy across the table with half-lidded eyes. "You and Nancy have a ball?"

Troy's eyes softened slightly with appreciation for Cressy's canny intervention. "Yeah, me and her went to a movie ... Elvis Presley."

"Presley! Sideburns and all ..." Cressy shivered grotesquely. "He gives me the creeps. Me, I like Debbie Reynolds and Dean Martin, somebody like that. There's class, not this lousy rock'n'roll stuff!"

Ma toyed with a remnant of egg and looked across at Cressy timidly. "I used to always like Joan Crawford and Clark Gable, nice folks like that," she offered.

Cressy considered thoughtfully. "Well, yeah, Ma, they been around a long time, but, sure, they got class."

"Goddam waste of time, if you ask me," Tom grunted.

Ma's eyes sharpened on her eldest son's face as he swore. She'd made it plain from the time they were small there'd be no cussing and damning at the table. She said nothing.

There was a long silence at the table as the five busied themselves with the remainder of the breakfast.

"Still goddam cold, ain't it?" Troy commented finally.

"We ain't havin' no more swearin' at the table!" Ma exploded. "I been tellin' the both of you that ever since you was able to talk, still you go at it!"

"Sorry, Ma," Troy dismissed the matter lightly. "Still, like I say, it sure ain't warmed up none."

"Won't be long now, come April and May," Tom observed. "Pretty soon now, God willin', we'll be gettin' our share of some rain and gettin' close to plantin' time."

"Gettin' thunder and lightning and maybe a couple of nice little ole twisters bouncin' across the plains, maybe," Troy threw in casually.

Cressy wrinkled her nose. "Them I can do without. What I'm waitin' for is summertime. It may come hot but I love it. It's the cold I hate. I wisht I could just curl up and sleep out the winter."

Troy glanced from her face to his brother. Tom was eyeing her closely and Troy watched covertly as Tom moistened his lips gingerly. There was a tug at Troy's lips. Sleep all winter with Cressy and there wouldn't be much left of Brother Tom come springtime!

"What you plannin' today?" Will turned and eyed his eldest son.

"Today? Gonna get in that cat and see what's kickin' up all the fuss."

"Still grindin'?"

"Yeah, sounds like some of them gears got out of line, but good!"

Troy shoved his chair back and dug down in the tight-mouthed pocket of the old levis for his crumpled cigarettes. Cressy took the one he offered across the table and Tom refused. Troy scratched the big kitchen match on his flank and leaned over until Cressy got her light, drew back and let the smoke come streaming from her nostrils. Troy lit up from the same flame and leaned back with a grunt.

"What's this I hear about Joe Ben Potter thinkin' about gettin' married again?" Troy asked.

Ma had started to rise to clear the table; now she sank back into her place and her eyes on Troy were wide with astonishment. "Our Reverend Potter?" she blurted. "The preacher?"

"Yeah, I was talkin' downtown with Billy Joe Everett. Says his ma was sayin' so."

"But, who on earth ..."

"Mrs. Dovely," Troy supplied, tipping his ash into the egg-encrusted plate.

"Martha Dovely! Well, I never in all my born days ..." Ma sat back, her hands on her hips, and regarded Troy with astonishment. "Why, Martha's ..." she faltered. "Well, I reckon she's 'round about his age, at that!"

Tom grinned. "Well, after all, Ma, there's no reason Joe Ben Potter shouldn't have somebody for himself. Mrs. Potter's been dead ... how long? Three, four years now? And Dovely's, let's see ... hell, he got killed in that tractor accident, must be eight, ten years back. I was still goin' to high school!"

Ma's brow furrowed. She went back down the half-forgotten pathway of the years. "Just about," she agreed. " 'Course," her eyes roamed around the family circle defiantly, "Martha Dovely's a fine person, a good, solid Baptist. And she's been workin' 'round the church a long time, helpin' out and all. Reckon that's how they became close. Reverend Potter now, well, he needs someone; I reckon as how we all need someone in this world."

"Sure thing." Tom's gaze went from his mother's thoughtful face to his father's weather-beaten, seamed hands clasped on the table before them all. His eyes rose to the face. The old man was sitting back, his head tilted slightly, his eyes almost closed. He's got everything taken care of for him, thank God, Tom thought, just the way it should be for his old age, sick and all. And that's right, as it should be. His hand groped under the screen of the table top and he found his wife's hands clasped in her lap. They were cold and there was no response. He squeezed them lightly but there was no change of expression on Cressy's face. Her eyes were lazy; she was looking across the table at Troy and there was a kind of speculation in her gaze.

Troy was busy mashing the cigarette end out in the untidy muck of his plate.

"I wish you wouldn't do that, Troy!" Ma snapped. "If I told you once I told you a hundred times, makes washin' up terrible. Sometimes, son, I don't think you ever listen to nothin', I declare!"

"I forgot, Ma," Troy returned blandly. "Reckon as how I clean forgot." He glanced across the table and winked and Cressy turned her head, looking away from him.

Tom moved his chair back and stretched to his feet. "Come on, boy, let's get goin'," he urged.

Troy grunted and hoisted his big frame from his place. He stood straight, raising his arms over his head, sucking his breath deep into his chest.

Ma's eyes narrowed on the tight clutch of the old levis almost directly in front of her eyes. They had turned a smoky pale blue with repeated washings and the seams and the edge of the fly were almost white and furry. She cleared her throat and glanced up at Troy's light-stubbled face. "If I was you, son, I'd be thinkin' about gettin' rid of them old pants. They're disgraceful. You got you a good pair you could be wearin'. Far as I can see, there ain't much left to them, if you was to ask me."

"I'm savin' the good ones for town, Ma," Troy protested.

"You sure wouldn't go to town in them tacky things," Cressy chuckled. "They'd be runnin' you in for indecent exposure or somethin'."

Troy shrugged. He knew what she meant. "Aw, ain't no reason for anybody here worryin'," he pointed out. "Nobody here but us."

"Reckon you're right, son," Will remarked quietly, his eyes puzzled, thoughtful, on the near-stranger who was his youngest. "There ain't never nobody 'round here but the family."

The Bannock men heaved and strained and pushed the disabled tractor inside the ramshackle frame building that had been the old barn and now served as a storeroom, seed supply, tool room, garage and general catch-all for the farm. Aside from the house itself, the barn and the pump house, the abandoned chicken shack and the obsolete outhouse leaning precariously near the open fields, there were no other buildings left on the place.

Troy sat on an upturned crate, his legs thrust wide in front of him as props, and cupped the cigarette in his greasy palm, eyeing the cobwebbed eaves. Down at his right the earthen floor was strewn with tractor innards and the stillness of the old barn was fluted with the whine of the wind and jabbed with the occasional strike of metal against metal as Tom worked somewhere under the bulk of the machine.

Troy sighed. That Rita'd been all right last night. Even thinking about her brought the tightening to his loins. He moistened his lips and rubbed his sweaty palm along the smoothness of the tight levis.

Tom wiggled his body out from under the tractor and rolled up into a sitting position. He brushed the hair back from his eyes and scowled up at his brother. "What the hell you think you're doin'? Just sittin' on your dead ass watchin' me do all the work?"

"Just been takin' a break, havin' a smoke, dad," Troy parried easily.

"Toss us one, kid." Tom rubbed his palms together, trying to work off the grit and oil.

Troy fished the pack from the waistband of the levis and tossed the single cigarette down to his brother. The paper book of matches fluttered close by. Tom lit the cigarette, handed up the matches and sat watching Troy with that damned distant smile on his face.

"What's so funny?"

"Funny?" Troy blinked. "Nothin's funny, I was just thinkin'."

"Yeah? About what?"

Troy eyed the slope of his brother's neck, the place where the thick hair curled inward. "You need a clippin'," he observed absently.

"Yeah, I know." Tom's fingers went back and he traced along the hairline. "Damn stuff grows like a weed. Get me a haircut when we go to town Saturday." He locked his heavy arms around his knees and regarded his brother curiously. "You still look like you know somethin' worth a laugh."

Troy dropped the cigarette and ground the stub into the floor with the toe of his shoe. "Just somethin' somebody told me in town last night," he countered vaguely. "Just a joke."

Tom expelled the smoke in a long stream, letting it flow out from his mouth like a great bluish tongue, curling at the tip. "I could stand a laugh," he invited.

"Oh, for God's sake, it ain't nothin'!" Troy shoved Rita from his mind and covered his face with the mask of detachment. "Just a story about how one guy says to the other guy, 'Say, I give my dog a physic this mornin' and he passes two worms this long.' " Troy measured out about six inches to show the length. "Other guy, he says, 'Hell, that's nothin', I give my dog a double physic this mornin' and he passes three cars and a truck!' " Troy's laugh burst brassily at the last.

Tom sat still, watching his brother with a puzzled expression. He ain't nothin' but a kid still, he thought, nothin' but a damn schoolboy, no matter how much of a build he's got on him!

Troy had sobered and he returned Tom's stare. "Why ain't you laughin'?" he demanded.

"I don't think it's funny, that's all," Tom grunted. "Sounds kinda silly, if you ask me."

"Well, I ain't askin' you for nothin'," Troy snapped.

"Don't be a sorehead, kid." Tom hunched himself to his knees. He got to his feet and leaned down to brush the dirt from the now soiled khakis.

"I ain't no sorehead," Troy barked. "You just ain't got no sense of humor, never did have." His eyes were hot on his brother. "Sometimes you'd think you was as old as Pa, the way you go 'round, frozen face and everything!"

Tom smiled indulgently. "Well, I ain't as old as Pa ... but I'm sure as hell a lot older'n you, by a damn sight." He laughed.

"I don't know nothin' you can do I can't do as well, better even!" Troy challenged.

"Perhaps." Tom crossed to the barn wall, shoved open the little door and peered outside. "Sure is gray out there, maybe we'll be gettin' some snow. Don't feel so cold as it did." He squinted and then the smile came. "Here comes Cressy, looks like she's runnin' the coffee break this mornin'." He stood holding the door open until she had pushed breathlessly through the opening.

She carried two cups in one hand, the old soot-stained coffeepot in the other. Her head was bound in a white scarf tied firmly under her chin. Tom reached for her waist but she twisted, slipping through his groping hands.

"Stop it, Tom! Can't you see I got my hands full!"

"That's what I was aimin' to do with mine, get 'em full." He laughed.

Cressy came straight across the floor toward Troy. "Yeah, well, there's times and places for everything!" she snapped back.

Tom followed his wife and reached out and took the pot and cups from her. He set them on the floor boards of the tractor. He shoved her hands aside and worked the tight knot of the kerchief loose, stripping the cloth from her head. With a free hand he cupped her chin and kissed her firmly, holding her head solid against her struggling efforts to free herself. "There," he crowed, stepping back, "you been kissed!"

Cressy wiped her mouth with the back of her hand. "Yeah," she grumbled.

He laughed and turned, reaching down for the cups and coffeepot. He handed a cup to Troy and made one for himself. "Shoo! It's hotter'n hell!"

"Ought to be, it's right off the stove!"

"Just right for me," Troy cradled the hot cup between his palms. "Hot, like I like it."

Cressy's eyes met his and they held for a moment. Once again the edge of something undefinable caught her, came unwarned and confusing. The blue of his eyes on her was cold, the whites pure and unbroken, despite the late hours of the night before. The steady impersonal coolness of his gaze betrayed the warmth of his easy smile on her and she shivered slightly.

"It's gettin' cold out here," Tom said, coming up behind her, putting his arm around her, hard against her breasts. "Maybe you best be gettin' on back to the warm house."

"No," she shook her head abruptly, "I'm all right. It was just a breeze or somethin'."

He took his arm away and hitched up his khakis. "Well, you two make talk while Papa goes outside and relieves the tension."

Cressy turned as he left and she and Troy watched him cross the open pan of the barn floor, push open the small door and step beyond their sight. The whine of the door closing died out and the place became startlingly still.

Cressy looked back at Troy, then took her eyes hastily away from his quickening gaze. "You want some more coffee?" She reached out and took the cup, going over to the tractor to refill it. As she gave it to him, his fingers caught at her wrist, closing on the flesh. Panic came surging up in her and she wrenched herself free.

"Keep your hands off me, Troy, you hear?" Her words were thick, her voice held low. She flashed a darting glance at the closed door across the space. She backed away a little. "I know you don't mean nothin' by foolin' around like that, only Tom might not understand. He might get to thinkin' somethin' else, if he was to come in and see you doin' somethin' like that!"

Troy sipped at his coffee, his eyes on her over the rim of the cup. He made no further attempt to come close to her.

She wandered nervously around the cavernous place, pausing now and then to reach out and absently finger some object hung from the nails on the wall, keeping her eyes resolutely from him.

"I kinda got you all bothered, huh?" he offered wickedly, his voice muffled in the hollow of the cup. "Kinda gets you all stirred up, don't it?"

She halted in her rounds and stared across the intervening space. He had that odd half smile on his face, his eyes steady on her. "You're nuts," she flung at him. "You talk like a damn fool."

He sat down, lolled back indolently on the box seat, the cup cradled in his big hands in his lap. "You think so?"

"You sure got a number-one opinion of yourself, Troy, I'll say that. It's too bad everybody don't feel quite the same way."

"I ain't interested in what everybody thinks," he grunted.

She came swiftly across the barn, stopped short and kept her distance. "Look, you're big; you're good-lookin' and you got some mighty big ideas, too. Only remember somethin' where I'm concerned, Troy, I got my man already. I ain't lookin' for nobody else, hear?"

"You love Tom?" he asked suddenly. "Do you, honest?"

The sharp effrontery of his open question shocked her into silence. Her eyes narrowed. It seemed as if her hands had taken on a life of their own. They went on opening and shutting without reason. Angered with them she shoved them deep in the back pockets of her jeans, curling her fingers into little tight-packed balls.

"Tom and me happens to be married," she stated coldly.

"Yeah, I know all that." Troy fished out a cigarette and devoted himself to the light. "He's my brother, too."

"I don't see what that's got to do with it, but you might try rememberin' the fact."

"Hell, I don't get much chance to be forgettin' it 'round here." Troy spoke half humorously through smoke as he held the lighted match in front of his lips.

Cressy took herself away from him. She walked slowly alongside the tractor, tracing along the edges of its parts with a thin, scarlet nail. "You better get somethin' straight, Troy. When your brother and me was married down in Dallas, that was the end of one kind of life for me, see? Out here I'm Mrs. Tom Bannock, and that's the way it is." She turned and faced him soberly, her chin raised, forcing her eyes to meet his derisive look. "I didn't want to come out here in the middle of nowhere to live, nothin' to do, nothin' to see but miles and miles of flat, empty, dried-up land. No trees, no water, no flowers, no grass, just sand and cold and heat and bugs and wind. Oh, I tried to get Tom to go somewheres else, some-wheres where we could have a life of our own, away from the family and all that. I wanted us to be alone, just us, in our own place...." She faltered and her eyes shifted around the reaches of the old barn. "Well"—she shrugged—"it didn't work that way, leastways, not yet."

She brought her attention back to his bemused face. "You're dead wrong about a lot of things you think you know everything about, Troy. 'Cause, you see, no matter whether Tom and me lives somewheres else, or right here on the place with Ma and Pa and you, we're married and there ain't no room for anybody thinkin' they can go playin' around or anything."

She flushed and crossed the barn floor and stood silently staring at an old discarded harness, bound to the uneven wall boards by a maze of gray cobwebs.

"You'll be gettin' away from here one of these days come fall when you go down to Austin, like you say," she said slowly. "That's good. It's right and you got the brains to go and do what you want." She turned and faced him. "Somebody's got to keep the place goin' and I reckon that's Tom's job. And ... where Tom is ... that's where I am, see, Troy?"

She caught her breath at the constant derisive smile plastered on his lips and she turned her head slightly, sending her gaze off into the shadows at the rear of the place.

"You asked me if I loved Tom...." Her voice trailed off. In a moment she looked directly at him and there was a sharp lift to her tone. "I know when I'm well off, Troy, I ain't changin' nothin', ain't allowin' nothin' to happen that could change anything. Yes, dammit, I love Tom."

Troy smoked and watched her with that thin veil of lazy amusement. When her talk had ended, he shrugged his shoul-ders elaborately, flicked the ash down at his side. "I was just askin'," he said calmly. "Wasn't no need to go makin' a whole goddam speech about it."

She came a little closer to him, her expression sharpening with tension, her eyes clouding faintly with sudden concern. "Troy, there ain't no need me kiddin' you. There's somethin' about you ... I don't know what it is ... it's nothin' like I ever felt before ... it's just I don't trust you much, not close up, not like this." She had said it with a rush and now she stumbled to a pause. "I'm askin' you as nice as I can not to be puttin' your hands on me, ever. Don't come too close to me."

Troy stared at her. Then he grinned and brought his long legs together, dropping the cigarette butt on the earth floor, crushing it with his heel. "I get you," was all he said.

She frowned at him, uncertain, then turned and walked back to the tractor. For a moment she eyed the open bowels of the thing vacantly, then she turned slowly and leaned her hip against the cold metal.

"I wonder if you do," she murmured thoughtfully. "I wonder." She drew no response from him, sitting with his back half turned to her. After a moment she brightened. "You can toss me one of them cigarettes," she suggested.

He turned and looked up at her and she saw his lazy eyes lingering as always on the swell of her blouse and the rush of blood darkened her face. All the things she had been saying, he hadn't paid any attention at all! The cut of the cigarette package reminded her suddenly she had brought her own. "Never mind," she said curtly, "I'll smoke my own."

"You can have one of mine, Cressy, if you want," he offered quietly.

"No thanks," she refused. "I'll stick to my own."

"Suit yourself."

Troy shoved his big frame off the box and ambled easily toward the tractor. Instinctively she moved to one side, holding the cigarette away and back from her side. Troy laughed, pausing directly in front of her, looking down on her with amused eyes.

"Lots of talk," he commented, "no action."

Cressy's breath caught as he moved closer. His big arm caught her waist harshly and he pulled her roughly to him. Before she could avert her head, he clamped his mouth down on hers, holding her in a viselike grip for the moment. Releasing her abruptly, he thrust her from him, laughed and turned his back on her, crossing to the machine.

Cressy's breath rasped. "What was you tryin' to prove?" she demanded.

"Just that, if I wanted to, I could ..." He chuckled.

"If Tom was to find out what his baby brother was up to ..."

He turned from the machine and smiled impishly. "Come on, Cressy, can't you take a joke? I didn't mean nothin'. I believe what you said. It's just you been bellyachin' for hours on all that crap, I just played games with you."

Suddenly her cheeks flamed. She realized that he meant what he said. He had already turned his back on her, dismissed her, and the incident was over in the instant. All the build-up she had given herself was nothing. He simply wasn't interested. She nervously dropped the cigarette and crushed out the coal with the toe of her shoe.

Troy was bent over the tractor engine, his arms down inside the hollow, working steadily. She watched the play of his muscles under the thin masking of the T-shirt and let her eyes trail down the ridging knobs of his spine that mounded along his back. The shirt was hiked up slightly above the waistband and she could see the glinting patch of hair in the small of his back. His legs seemed ready to come bursting through the worn denim.

Cressy moved slowly. She ran her hand over her brow and pushed away the straggling strands of hair that threatened to fall. Taking the scarf from the workbench she tied it in place and crossed to the small door at the end of the barn. Hesitating she looked back to where he worked. As if the message had communicated itself across the clearing, he straightened suddenly and looked her way. He ran his greasy hands down his thighs and then hitched his pants a little.

"Don't go runnin' off mad," he chuckled.

Her lips parted, but she changed her mind. He was nothing but a larking kid, having fun with everybody in the world. Irritably she shunted the door open with the butts of her palms. There was a sharp agonized whine as the door closed.

Troy grinned. Women! Where they got some of their ideas, he'd never know. Cressy was a good kid, the best, she was just all screwed up. Maybe, he thought, as the years went on and on, Tom could kinda shake her down into place, maybe not. He shrugged and dismissed them and their damfool problems. Wasn't no skin off him one way or the other.

# CHAPTER FIVE

I t was the sound of Harry relieving himself that brought Rita Karnes's eyes open. The small shaft of bright sunlight filtering through the crack between the worn shade and the windowsill stabbed at her face, blinding her for the moment. Irritable, she rolled away from the intrusion, twisting her body sharply, until her quickening gaze fell on the open maw of the bathroom door. Harry was still at it; from the sound of him he must have had a gallon last night.

In a moment he was done and the plumbing of the old apartment house groaned and sucked as it flushed away the discard. At the sound of the soft scuff of his bare feet on the floor, Rita dropped her lids and feigned sleep.

Harry Marvel came to the door to the bedroom and stood there looking across at the humped body beneath the table of bedclothes. He was naked and she could see him quite plainly.

He stood there for some time, his blunted nails digging absently into the curly wire of the reddish mat that eagled itself over his thick chest, stood staring toward the bed. Absently his hand dropped lower and he picked the residue of lint from the deep pock of his navel and he flicked it into the room. As he did so, he moved forward, coming close to the side of the bed, bending forward slightly, his head cocked as he listened to the measure of her breathing.

"If you got some goddam idea you're makin' me believe you're still asleep, you can can it," he chopped bluntly. "I sure as hell know by this time if you're sleepin' or not."

Rita groaned. She rolled to her back and brought her arm across her eyes and sighed heavily. Sometimes, when she woke in the mornings like this, her body seemed weighted, her legs numbed by the hours on end on the drive-in paving.

Harry Marvel made no move to get back into the bed. He simply watched her. The only change in his face was the faint narrowing of his eyes.

Finally she took her arm down and opened her eyes and looked up at him sourly.

"What time's it gettin' to be?" she whispered huskily.

He shrugged his heavy shoulders and splayed his big hands away from his thick hips. " 'Bout noon, I reckon."

She groaned again and worked the inside of her mouth, trying to rid it of the scummy aftereffects of the gin she had shared with Troy Bannock. "Well," she grunted, "reckon I best be gettin' up." Her eyes found his face and she stared at him distastefully. "You'd do me a helluva favor, Harry, if you'd shut the door when you're takin' a leak, that's the least you can do. It sounds lousy."

"Just doin' what comes naturally." Harry grinned. He came very close to the bed and stared down at her. "How come you was so late gettin' back to the place last night?"

Rita had her eyes closed again and now she bit on the inside of her lower lip. Without opening her eyes she spoke. "Just went along with one of the girls, had a couple of snorts."

"One of the girls, eh?"

She opened her eyes and the frown deepened the cleft between her brows. "Sure ... You got any objections?"

Harry Marvel suddenly sat down on the edge of the bed. He leaned forward and drew down the sheet, baring her full breasts.

His crusty fingers touched the roseate nipple gently. "Ain't never objected to you runnin' around with a couple of girl friends, have I?" he asked silkily.

"Well," she offered defensively, "that's the way it was."

He caught the nipple between his thumb and forefinger and pinched once, hard. "Just see it keeps that way, hear?"

She cried out, twisted sharply and pushed at his thick arm. "Harry, goddammit! You're hurtin'!"

"Not real hurtin'."

"That's what you think!"

Harry Marvel hunched forward a little. Now she caught the sourness of his breath and turned her head aside.

"You stink like some brewery!"

Harry shrugged. "Just a few beers last night ... With one of the boys," he added meaningfully.

"A few gallons, smells like."

Harry smiled slowly. His hands had opened now and were moving very quietly over her breasts and now they moved down, drawing the sheet farther, and he stroked the round of her belly. Of all the things he loved in the world, nothing pleased Harry Marvel so much as looking at her stripped like that, most beautiful goddam sight in the world. "You got a nice body, you know that? It's kind of soft and hard, all at the same time."

"It's damned tired this mornin'," she qualified.

Harry's breathing sharpened. He jerked away the sheet and exposed her completely, his eyes feeding on the length of her, on the familiar yet always exciting lines of her against the rumpled sheet.

"Harry, no! Not this mornin' please, I'm so goddam bushed!"

Harry Marvel came alongside her now, coming up close to her, putting his thick hairy arm across her breasts, catching her under her ribs and drawing her close. "Been a long time," he murmured against her flesh. "Too damn long."

Feebly she tried to resist but her strength was depleted. He had caught her firmly and now his free hand explored the hidden recesses of her, bringing the low flame within her to a responding burst. Automatically she came to him, slipping her arms around his muscled back, catching at him with the sudden, sharp hunger that lay always just waiting in her. In a moment all that had brought her to Harry Marvel that first time reasserted itself all over again. She did not feel the harshness of his hands on her, the sandpapering scrape of his face against her flesh, the quick, plunging, demanding drive of him. She felt nothing but the empty striving for fulfillment, the always seeking demand of herself with him.

When he was done with her, Harry Marvel took himself from her side. For a long moment he stood again at the side of the bed and his smile was sure, knowing. She lay turned slightly away from him, one arm flung out toward the far edge of the bed, and the only indication of her living was the slight rise and fall of her breasts, the slow pumping of her belly.

Harry Marvel crossed the room and felt among the discarded clothing for his underthings. In a matter of minutes he had dressed himself and crossed to the door to the hallway.

"Harry?"

Her low call stopped him and he turned.

"Where you goin' now?"

"Where the hell you think I'm goin'?" he snorted. "This here's my day to open up the rink, ain't it?"

"You comin' back for supper?"

"How the hell I know what I'm gonna be doin' by then?"

The opening of the door, the sharp slam of the battered panel put an end to his talk. Rita sighed. She lay curved in the bed for some time, simply fixing the door with her dulled, tired eyes. Stretched out like this, her body fluid with fatigue, Rita allowed her mind to have its own way. She went back down through the years and idly toyed among the relics. She remembered how it was so long ago. She recalled the farm and the old man and her ma and all the kids, patched and starved and livin' in the dirt from drought to drought without any promise, without any hope.

Sometimes, in those rare moments when she let her thinking run free, she reckoned maybe she oughtn't to have pulled out like that, gone skittering off into town, leaving the rest of them to work out their problems.

Only, after her daddy had found out about Clancy Williams and how he'd been the first, after that awful beating and the days after days of Bible reading and down-on-the-knees praying for forgiveness for something that didn't concern them at all, something that hadn't seemed at all like a praying thing to her, well, she couldn't take any more of that. She couldn't take it and she couldn't stop the wanting someone like Clancy all over again. So the best thing had been to pack up and clear out, to get off by herself and make out the best she could.

For a long time, really, there had been no Clancys in her life. She had reckoned maybe it was all the praying and all the fussing that kind of stuck in her craw after all and kind of made her put aside that feeling inside her those times she saw some guy, had a couple of beers with someone who got to looking at her, she knew how.

And then there'd been Harry Marvel, come up out of nowhere one night, big, strong, bull Harry and his looking at her like that! She could remember right now, just how it was.

She'd gotten a job hashing at a drugstore counter. The pay was lousy and she'd gotten damn sick of looking over the counter at pimply-faced kids with their sports shirts open to their navels, their little medals on silver chains and their thin, already fading tattoos. She'd gotten damn sick and tired of them making what they thought were smart remarks and trying to be the men they weren't.

Then she'd gotten out of the dry town and found that counter job in the wet town and somehow that began to change everything. She hadn't been two days on the new job before she'd met up with Harry Marvel and suddenly they'd been alone in his pick-up out there in the hot, dusty, blowing field and Clancy had happened all over again and Harry'd put a stop to all that hungering that went on inside her morning, noon and night.

She twisted now and glanced toward the bright strip at the bottom of the crooked shade. She'd been surprised when Harry'd gotten himself all steamed up that night she had a beer with the salesman; Harry'd really thrown her for a loop when he'd gotten her out there in the cotton field alone and right in the middle of their making love had said he wanted her living with him, just for him alone, nobody else.

She smiled thinly at the sunlight strip. After almost five years now, she knew damn well why. She knew his tempers and his strength and the fear that rode constant in her when his face grew mottled and those lips thinned down and his big hands began to ache to take hold of her. Harry Marvel didn't own much, but what Harry owned he kept, all for himself. It'd take a helluva man to get the skating rink away from Harry, 'cause he had it tight and legal and proper. And with her, well, he had her, too, she knew that, not legal or anything, but she was his woman and that was that.

Rita stirred and slid from the bed, cutting across the room to the window and raising the shade. Down along the alley she could see the usual bunch of parked delivery trucks, the usual pile of ugly, battered cardboard cartons and crates stacked up outside the rear doors of the stores. Directly across the rearing stories of the county jail loomed as an ever-present reminder. She wondered why she ever looked out of the damn window; what she saw out there was no prize package.

At the bathroom sink Rita leaned forward and examined the tell-tale crow's-feet already edging at the corners of her eyes, saw the faint shadow of the etching lines at the corners of her mouth. She was getting along, she thought heavily, almost twenty-nine already! A few more years of this and there wouldn't be anything left!

Reaching for the toothbrush and paste, she was conscious again of the lousy, dirty taste in her mouth. Brushing, she let her mind play on Troy Bannock. He was nothing but a kid, really, even if he was maybe twenty or so. She reckoned she had no right putting her hands on him at all, a nice, clean kid like that. Only … She stopped suddenly and reached down, resting her weight on her palm on the sink edge, the toothbrush thrust through her fingers like a cigarette-holder. Her eyes asked the questions of her image in the glass, covered over with the hurting, grabbing possession of the hands of Harry Marvel, the fumbling, feeling, scoring of a boy she could barely remember named Clancy Williams.

It was funny, in a way, looking back on last night, remembering Troy Bannock, how him and Clancy Williams kind of merged together somehow; how Troy could have been Clancy and Clancy could have come back all over again and been Troy. She stared and finally went on brushing her teeth, working on the damage, getting ready for another day.

# CHAPTER SIX

Tom and Troy had worked in the barn Thursday without a break, without a word between them, other than grunted requests for tools or pointing out places for work. Only the sounds of tools against metal or an occasional grunt from one of them broke the surface of silence. Tom worked underneath the tractor, with only his legs thrust out in view. Troy had sidled up over the hood, until he was balanced on the ball of his hips, giving him complete freedom to work with his hands down inside the block.

This was the scene when Cressy went through the small door with the afternoon coffeepot and the cups in her hands. Carefully she made her way across the space, picking her way through the scattered parts of the machine, crossing to the long makeshift workbench covered with tools, nuts and bolts and parts.

She set the coffeepot down gingerly, laid out the cups and turned. Troy's buttocks loomed before her, mounded and solid, with his long, firm legs dangling down from his awkward position. He had not heard her; he went right on working without a pause.

She crossed quietly around the end of the machine and came close to her husband's legs. With the toe of her shoe she nudged him gently.

"For God's sake, watch what you're doin'!" The legs thrashed and the voice magnified in the recesses of the metal.

She grinned and nudged him again, a little more persuasively this time.

"Goddammit! I said cut it out!" The legs snaked underneath the old tractor and in a moment Tom came wiggling out from his place angrily. "Hell, Troy, can't you see ..."

"Hi."

Tom's anger dissipated instantly before her smile and the sheepishness came over his face. He scrambled out from under the machine and pulled himself straight, brushing at his trousers.

"Nothin' gonna do 'em much good, but an old-fashioned wash," she laughed.

He reached out and took her by the shoulders and bent forward carefully, kissing her lightly. "You bring coffee?"

"It's over there." She nodded. "On the bench."

He pulled his shirt open, yanking the tails from inside his trousers as he went around the machine. She watched as he poured a cup, smiled at his mock, silent toast to her. She came quickly around the hulk of the old machine and up close to him, slipping her arm around his waist, laying her cool palm against his chest.

"You know somethin'?" she said low.

He caught her up close to him. "Know what?"

She closed her eyes and let the feel of him come soaking through to her. "I love you, Tom.... Don't ever forget that." Her eyes opened and she found herself staring at the hump of Troy in front of them. He had apparently not heard her come, had not heard them talking together. Her clutch around her husband tightened imperceptibly and she turned, burying her face against the coarse hair of his chest, circling his neck with her arm. "No matter what happens, ever," she murmured, "I love you completely, with all of me."

He fought to keep the coffee balanced. He pressed her gently from him, grinning. Then he pulled from her grasp and crossed to where his brother worked. He poked the rear end sharply. "Hey, Troy!"

The legs knifed and in a cloud of muffled curses Troy emerged from the gaping hole, swiveled on his belly and glared at his brother. "What the hell you want now!"

"Coffee time."

With a grunt Troy rolled his body into a sitting position. "Well, let's have a cup." He rubbed his palms together roughly, then slid them down his thighs, trying to wipe off the grease.

Cressy had turned her back to them, and was pouring the coffee when Tom's bland, edgeless words brought her to a pause, her eyes lifting to fix on a nail on the wall.

"Get your ass down and get your own coffee."

Troy shrugged elaborately. He slid forward, letting his legs dangle until his feet came to the earthen floor. Pushing forward he straightened and came abreast of his brother.

Cressy was silent as she handed him the cup, averting her eyes from his curious gaze. She turned and walked over to her husband's side, carefully slipping her arm around his waist loosely.

"You make a real nice couple," Troy pronounced smoothly. "All homey-like, real domestic."

"That's the way it should be." She smiled faintly.

"Yeah, I reckon that's how it is."

Tom and Cressy walked idly toward the little door. In front of it Tom put his arms around her and tilted her face up to his. His kiss was gentle and sure. As he drew away from her, Cressy's glance drifted past his shoulder and she saw Troy at the bench. On his face was a slight, half-amused smile and there was the faintest lift to his brows. As their eyes met, he pursed his lips and thrust his head forward a little. His wink brought the sudden flush to Cressy's face.

Tom felt the little stiffening that came to her. He stepped back, his hands still on the soft flesh of her upper arms, and eyed her anxiously. "You gettin' cold out here. I plumb forgot you didn't have no coat or nothin' on around you."

"I'm all right, Tom, really."

"Nix on that." He stepped forward and thrust open the little door. "You get yourself back to the house. You shouldn't be out here in the drafts and all."

"I'm fixin' to go. Honest, Tom, I'm perfectly all right." A sudden flare of irritation spread through her. "I wish you'd stop fussin' over me!"

"Git!" He shoved her from him, slapping her lightly on the round of the tight blue jeans. He stood smiling in the doorway as she went running. across the clearing to the house. He stayed as he was until the distant report of the slamming back screen reached his ears.

Troy had poured the last of the coffee and stood still, smoking a cigarette. Tom came back slowly and reached over, hefting the pot, shaking it to see if there was any coffee left. When he found there was none, he glanced sideways at his brother and the corners of his mouth tightened.

"You always manage to suck up the last of everything, don't you?"

"Sorry, I wasn't thinkin'."

"That's one of your special talents, not thinkin'," Tom grunted.

Troy fished another cigarette from the pack, lit it from the stub of the first one. He peered through the ballooning smoke at his brother. "What's eatin' on you, Tom? You been ridin' me a lot lately. Now you're at it again."

"Lots of things," Tom snapped. He moved ahead, going to the side of the tractor, stood staring down into the gaping bowels of the engine.

"I don't get it," Troy's eyes rested cloudily on his brother.

Tom said nothing for the moment. Then he idled along the length of the tractor. He laid his palm on the cold metal and turned back to Troy. "Sometimes I get the feelin' you don't give a damn about nothin', Troy, despite what you keep sayin' about school and all that."

Troy flushed. He took a quick, nervous drag on the cigarette and waved his hand to encompass the whole of the place. "What's there to give a damn about 'round here?" he inquired glibly. He spat over his shoulder. "It's all right for you; you're different from me. You got Cressy and you like spendin' your life here on the farm and that's that. You ain't lookin' for kicks, and you don't get no kicks."

Tom frowned. "I don't follow."

Troy hurled the cigarette in the dirt, spun on his heel and ground out the coal. He shoved his hands down deep in his hip pockets and teetered on his heels, staring up into the spider-webbed eaves of the barn. "I hate this place," he confessed quietly. "I reckon I always hated it. I hate lookin' out across the wide open fields; I hate grubbin' 'round for the lousy crops; I hate there bein' no place to go except to town, nobody to see; I hate the whole set-up."

Tom's brows lifted in surprise. "It ain't as if you was goin' to stay forever on the place," he reminded him slowly. "Come next fall, you'll be goin' down to Austin, studyin', doin' whatever you want."

"That's way next fall."

"Four, five months more."

"Yeah." Troy was gloomy.

Tom's voice softened. Sometimes he reckoned as how he forgot the kid was just a kid, that time is a big thing, especially when a person has so much of it ahead, even though it might look like so little. "Nobody's tryin' to make you do nothin' you don't want, Troy. Why, kid, you got it made. After you're done with schoolin', well, you can do pretty much whatever you like. You got the brains, even I got to admit that, you'll be able to do just about anything."

"In the meantime, I gotta go on sittin' on my can out here in the middle of nowheres," Troy's words were surly.

"Balls!" Tom's anger flared. "You're just actin' like a baby. Everytime somethin' don't go just right for you, you start squallin'."

Troy sobered. He stared at his brother, seeing him now covered with grease and grit, seeing the powerful set of the body, the big knowing hands hooked in the belt loops of the khakis, just hanging there waiting to be called back to work. "What's all this gonna get you?" he demanded suddenly. "How come you don't care nothin' for gettin' away?" Troy glanced around the barn and snorted. He remembered what Cressy had said about hopin' maybe they'd be somewhere else, her and Tom, someday. "The farm! What's it get you in the long run? Look at Pa … Why, hell, he ain't an old man, not really. There's men all over the place older'n Pa, a helluva lot older, and they're still grubbin' out a miserable bastard existence farmin'. And Pa … all he can do is sit around, day in and day out, sit around doin' nothin', not carin' about nothin', just sittin', waitin' to die off."

Tom bit the edge of his underlip. "That's just one of them things." He shrugged helplessly. "If Pa's arthritis hadn't come on, he'd be workin', grubbin' like you say. Only he can't. It's just one of them things you just got to put up with when it happens, is all. Pa knows it.… He ain't so happy about it either, remember that."

"You got all the answers down pat now, ain't you, Tom, all squared away."

"No, I ain't got all the answers, that seems to be your goddam department. I just know there's no sense gettin' riled up over things you can't be helpin'."

Troy hesitated. He cleared his throat and his gaze went out beyond Tom to some distant point in the shadows. "Sometimes, Tom, when I'm sacked up, layin' there listenin' to the goddam wind howlin' 'round the house, sometimes in the summers when the sun's borin' down on the fields, when the sweat's blindin' your eyes so's you can hardly see the furrows between the rows, I get scared 'cause something like what happened to Pa might happen to you."

Tom stared at him. "You're worryin' about me? About maybe I might conk out along the way?"

"Yeah, I worry about you." Troy came forward a little and his eyes were intent on his brother's face. "Only, it ain't all you I'm worryin' about. Suppose somethin' happened to you. Where's that leave me? Stuck on my ass for the rest of my life right here, ain't that right? That'd be me, walled up inside the lousy place, spendin' my life like you're doin', walkin' up and down the goddam rows, watchin' for rain, scared as hell about the hail could wreck the crop, hopin' sometimes yes, sometimes no, a sonofabitchin' tornado'll come steamin' up out of the south and blow the whole works to kingdom come!" Troy choked on the last. He spat suddenly and turned away from the startled eyes before him. "You're goddam right, I worry. I'm worried 'cause if somethin' like what happened to Pa happened to you I'd be screwed, not just for now, not for tomorrow, not next month ... for my whole goddam life!"

Tom glanced down, troubled, tracing a haphazard circle in the soft dirt on the barn floor. "I suppose you reckon you're the only one who ever gets them thoughts," he said quietly. "Most farmin' men goes through wantin 'to quit ... every now and then."

"Crap." Troy's shoulders set. "They're just talkin'. They'd be up the creek without the paddle if they wasn't farmin'. Take a look at you, what the hell would you do, if all of a sudden there was none of this, no barn, no house, no tractor, no more fields?"

Tom looked up and then let his gaze move slowly around the barn. Somehow he'd never thought too much about it. From the time he'd been old enough to walk, this had been his world. There was no other world that mattered, that even existed. Cocking his head he measured the length of the old familiar wall, his eyes catching on the obsolete farming implements left over from his father's time, from his grandfather's time. What would he do, like Troy said, if all of a sudden this came to an end? If all of a sudden the Bannock place folded up, was blown away, was no more, what then? The smile of knowledge was slow in coming, but it came.

"I reckon I'd get me a job on some other place," Tom said simply. "Wouldn't be the same, but there'd be the land, the sky and the wind, the work I know. Nothin' really changes the land."

Troy turned and studied his brother. Tom's look was level. Troy knew things were just that simple for Tom, that Tom asked for no more than the things he had just said, that here was Tom's life, as complete as it ever would be, that what lay beyond the reaches of the sections were of no interest particularly to him. Troy touched his lips gingerly with the tip of his tongue.

"And what about Cressy? If somethin' was to happen to you, what about her?"

"Cressy?" Tom blinked.

"Yeah, Tom ... what happens to Cressy, your woman?" There was almost a shade of triumphant insolence in Troy's tone.

"How do you mean? I don't get you." There was a faint edge of suspicion in Tom's voice.

"There's lots you don't get sometimes, Tom. You ever take a good look at Cressy without them blinders of yours on? She ain't no farm girl. Hell, man, she's from Dallas; she's used to the big city and things to do, places to go and see." Troy grunted. "Sure, everything's okay now, so long as you're all right, so long as there's food on the table and everything's workin', out all right. Only, suppose something happens to you like what happened to Pa? Suppose, bingo! something happens and Cressy's got nothing more to look forward to but takin' care of you, feedin' you and wet-nursin' you for the rest of your life, like Ma does with Pa?"

"You're talkin' crazy, Troy. Cressy's my wife, like Ma is Pa's. There ain't nobody else, never would be. Cressy's mine. She'd stick."

Troy simply stood there, watching his brother. He saw the sudden shadows of concern, knew he'd raked up something that had never occurred to Tom.

Tom leaned against the workbench and swallowed the tightness from his throat. "You got a lot to learn, kid," he said slowly. "Trouble is right now you got nothin' but good times and dames on your mind. You reckon that's all there is. You reckon that's all the dames want, too, good times and all. Only, there's a difference. Well, that's somethin' you'll be learnin' for yourself one of these days. There's dames and dames. The kind you play with on the back seat of a car ain't the kind you wind up takin' home for a missus."

"Yeah ... maybe."

Tom frowned. Troy shouldn't ought to be talking like this. After all, Cressy was his wife; she wasn't like one of them town women! She was his wife and she had her place, come good or bad. He tried once again.

"Look, kid, there ain't nothing wrong in havin' a good time. Hell you're young and healthy; you're pretty strong and I reckon as how some dames think you're all right. That's good.... Have a good time, get all you can. We all done it at your age. Only, havin' a good time ain't really livin', kid. The livin' comes along later, when you're ready, you'll see, like me and Cressy. We got a life together, not just a good time. Whatever comes we stick together."

"Nuts!"

Tom straightened, his face darkening. "You ask Cressy some-time, see what she says. She'll tell you the same thing, you'll see."

"Maybe." Troy's words were barely audible. "Maybe she'll tell me different."

The crack of Tom's fist snapped through the stillness of the barn like a pistol shot. Troy, totally surprised by the sudden attack, reeled back and fell heavily, the dust spurting like jets of tawny smoke from under the solid impact of his big body. Tom moved swiftly, his fists clenched, and stood over his brother, his face mottled with rage.

"You been askin' for a pop in the mouth for a long time, kid! Times you been talkin' just a little too free!"

Troy made no sound. He reached up and wiped away the small trickle of blood with the back of his hand and shook his head slightly, trying to clear away the fog.

"You get up and I'll beat your brains out!" Tom stormed. "You ain't been usin' 'em lately anyhow!"

With a grunt Troy moved suddenly, not up, but sideways. His long powerful arms caught at his brother's legs, seizing them at the knees, and he jerked with all his strength. The older man toppled down across the twisting body. For a moment the dust cloud rose angrily around the struggling, grunting men, mask-ing them with a choking, blinding dirt shroud. In a second both men had broken free and come scrambling to their feet. Cagily they circled each other, alert for the sudden unguarded opening.

Troy balanced almost daintily on his toes. His big chest pulsed with his strained breathing and his eyes never left the slowly-advancing shorter hulk of his brother.

It was Tom who again struck the blow. His right fist tore hammer-hard against the side of Troy's head, throwing him off balance, propelling him with force against the blocking machinery.

Troy braced himself against the shocking impact. He used the solid backing to advantage, hurling his big body with a thrust. He laced into Tom with both fists flying, the blows landing indiscriminately, striking the smaller, heavier man on head and body without direction or purpose. There was a sucking, solid impact as a fist found an unguarded belly, a sickening crunch as bone met cartilage. There were no other sounds, no words, no curses; the only sounds in the place were the solid telling blows as flesh met flesh and the quick, sharp rasp of their panting.

Perhaps it was the slight difference of the few years between them. Or, perhaps, it was Troy's fighting in the high tide of youth and fighting for fighting's sake. The battle came to an end with the startling suddenness of its beginning. Troy threw a vicious left that caught Tom's cheekbone and he followed it with a right that caught near the eye.

Tom went staggering back, striking the tractor body with his full weight. There was an instant of shocked silence, followed by a drawn, low moan. Tom gripped the edge of the machinery desperately, his head erect, his eyes closed, his face cut and streaked with blood. He battled doggedly to hold on, shaking his head, struggling to get his bearings, to shake the strands of hair from his eyes. Then, in front of his brother's frozen gaze, Tom let go and crumpled to the floor with a long, relaxed kind of sigh. He lay there staring blindly ahead, the blinking of his lashes the only sign of life.

Troy swallowed and ran his hand back over his hair. His palm was bloody when he brought it down. Sharp fear came racing through him and he dropped to his knees and reached for Tom.

The "No!" ground harshly through Tom's clenched teeth. Drawing his knees up close to his belly, Tom summoned all his strength and rolled over until he was facing the tractor, his back humped against Troy.

Troy remained helplessly on his knees in the dirt. He still had his hand extended toward Tom. He tried once again to force a swallow through his sore throat muscles. The fight was all gone now; all the pent-up, bursting emotion of the moment was spent. He bent forward and put his hand gently on the knob of Tom's shoulder.

"Hey, fella ... Tom, you hurt bad?"

There was an answering quiver from the hunched-up body. Tom jerked convulsively and pulled his shoulder from the touch. "Just get the hell outta here, get away from me!" he groaned.

"I'll get Ma, Cressy...."

"Get out, goddammit! Don't get nobody, just get out and lemme alone!"

"But if you're hurt bad ..."

"Take more'n a punk like you to hurt me bad," Tom grunted. "I'll be okay, dammit, just get the hell outta here."

Troy backed away awkwardly on his knees. He groaned softly as he got to his feet. He looked helplessly around the barn. There wasn't anything he could do. He took a couple of experimental steps. Every joint, every bone, every muscle he owned was a mass of aches, throbbing under the punishment.

He thought of water. He'd get some water and wash their faces and clean off some of the blood. God, if Ma or Cressy was to come in now there'd be holy hell to pay!

Troy crossed swiftly to the barn door, opened it and peered out. The brilliant cold sunlight smote his aching eyes. The late March sun had no warmth, no friendliness. He glanced across the yard anxiously. There was no sign of life.

Quickly he slipped through the door and darted toward the pump. Sticking his head under the spout he worked the handle vigorously, letting the spitting, gathering icy stream cascade over his neck and shoulders, soaking the T-shirt, lancing along the flesh of his battered ribs.

Troy filled the bucket and lugged it hurriedly back into the barn. Nobody had caught sight of his flight; he was sure of that. He paused and listened. There had been a grunt from the direction of the tractor, no moaning or anything like that, just a grunt. As he came around the end of the machine, he found Tom had gotten to his feet. He stood wavering, using the vehicle as a prop. His hands were up over his face, the knuckles skinned raw.

"I ... I brought some water, Tom," he offered in a low voice. "Best get some of that gunk off else you'll scare hell outta Ma and the others."

Tom took his hands down. Troy caught his breath sharply and stepped back instinctively. There was a look akin to murder in his brother's eyes.

"I thought I said to get the hell outta here," Tom muttered hoarsely. "I meant get the hell out, too." He stepped forward. "Maybe you want some more of the same. Don't you ever learn nothin'?"

"Sure, sure thing, Tom." Troy blinked. "It was only the water. You ought to clean up some."

"Yeah."

Troy gritted his teeth. It was no use sayin' anything to Tom now, a waste of time to try and put back things right. He turned and moved off toward the door.

"Hey, you!"

Troy stopped but did not turn back. His eyes fastened on a snag of stick on the floor and he waited, a little lick of concern flitting down through him.

"You best take Ma on down to the Corners. She wants some stuff." There was an odd half pause. "I'm gonna be busy," Tom finished lamely.

Troy turned and looked back questioningly.

"Yeah, busy." He wiped his mouth. "Well, get the hell outta here, go take Ma down to the store. For God's sake, you want all of 'em pilin' out here, makin' all kinds of fuss over nothin' but an argument?" He faltered and his voice hardened slightly. "This ain't none of their business, see? It's our business, yours and mine."

"Okay."

Tom's eyes narrowed. "Get rid of that goddam T-shirt. Tell 'em you tore it on the machine or somethin'."

"Who you tellin' ..."

Tom moved painfully, suddenly, moved to the bench and took down the big wrench. He eyed his brother unemotionally. "You start horsin' around, Troy boy, and you're headin' for trouble." His words were icy. "I ain't in the mood for no goddam kid no more. I don't mind tellin' you right now I'd get me a powerful lot of pleasure just splittin' that thick head of yours wide open!"

Troy swallowed. "Don't get your balls in an uproar," he grumbled. "I'm goin'."

The sound of footsteps on the hard earth outside forced Tom to move. He went to the door of the barn and pushed it open. Troy's car jolted back with a spurt, scuffing rubber from the tires as he threw it into low and leaned heavily on the wheel. Tom could see he'd changed his clothes, washed up. The machine careened in a half-circle, its rear end skidding far to the right, then swinging precariously back to settle in line as the car reached the main road. There was a momentary pause, another scuffing spurt, and the roar rose loud, then went fading off as the car raced down the pavement toward town.

The thought came now to Tom that Troy had taken off without Ma, after he promised to take her to town. The scowl chopped into the smooth flesh of his face. He glanced toward the old pile of the house. Cressy had come out on the small landing of the porch and she stood with her eyes on him, waiting for him to come, her thin blouse riffling in the sharp wintry breeze.

Tom let his eyes remain on her. This was Cressy, his wife, the woman he loved, closer to him than all the rest put together, now and always. Yet the thing that Troy had hinted, that Cressy might think differently, the stupid, idiotic thing that had triggered the senseless fight, it stayed with him, too, cored in his mind.

Tom finally hitched up the khaki trousers with his wrists. He made his way across the yard to clean up and take Ma to the Corners. He limped slightly and his head was down. At the foot of the wooden steps he glanced up. Cressy's eyes were on him and there was concern in them. She made no move to come to him, to say anything. It was only as he plodded up the steps that she came forward and reached out to touch her hand to his arm as he neared the landing.

He paused, searching her face curiously, as if he wanted suddenly to find a reassurance in her, and then he opened the back door and took himself from her touch.

"I'd just like to be left alone for a while," he said quietly. "I'd just like to be by myself."

# CHAPTER SEVEN

Troy lolled back on the stool, stretching his legs out lazily on the narrow curbing that bordered the drugstore fountain. His fingers poked around the remnants of potato chips on the plate, seeking out the larger bits which he popped into his mouth absently. Bored, he let his gaze drift down the length of the counter. His attention was snagged suddenly by the small, oval-shaped face of a girl beyond the fat one. She had long dark hair and it framed perfectly the pale delicate face, bringing out the cream of her skin, the white of her teeth. She moved her hand as Troy's interest quickened; she reached for a glass of water and he saw the ring. Hell, that's the way it was; all the good ones got themselves married right off.

The fall of the hand on his shoulder startled him and he pulled his legs in and threw his head back, looking up at the tall, rangy figure standing at his side. "Oh, hi-ya Billy Joe, what's up?"

"Nothin'." Billy Joe Everett slid his lanky frame on the adjoining stool. He rubbed his eyes hard with the butts of his palms and, when he took them down, he glanced at Troy's plate and the empty Coke glass. "You been eatin'?"

"Yeah, I was hungry."

"I reckon you was," Billy Joe retorted dryly. He glanced at his friend curiously. "How come you're in town today? Kinda early, too, ain't it?"

"Just reckoned I'd come."

Billy Joe's eyes widened now and he came forward a little, staring at Troy's face. "Holy cow! what happened to you, man? You fall down or somethin'?"

Troy shrugged. His big hands went out and he began to revolve the plate slowly. "Just had me an argument."

Billy Joe licked his lips and swallowed. "Some character here in town?"

Troy wagged his head slightly. "My brother, … Tom."

"Tom? Tom, he beat you up?"

Troy's lips thinned and he stared straight ahead, watching the skinny, pimply-faced blonde serving down the way. "Wouldn't say he beat me up," he retorted lamely.

"Sure looks like it!"

"He don't look so good."

"How come?"

"How come what?"

"How come all the fightin' with you-all?"

"Nothin'." Troy shrugged. "Nothin' important."

"Jesus, Troy! Guys don't go 'round makin' hamburgers out of each other without somethin' bein' wrong!"

Troy spun on his stool and scowled at Billy Joe. "You ever try mindin' your own business?"

Billy Joe took the measure of the angry face before him. Then he seemed to withdraw behind an invisible wall. There was a sudden hurt look in his eyes. "Okay, man, okay. I was only askin'."

"Keep your askin' to yourself."

Billy Joe winced. If he hadn't known this big bastard since they was kids together, he'd like to add another cut or two right here and now on that mush. He shrugged and looked away. "Okay, buddy, if that's the way you want it."

"That's the way I want it."

The silence came creeping around them. They sat mired in their own uncomfortable trap, listening intently to the sounds drifting across the big drugstore, pinning their attentions away from each other, watching the constant coming and going of the customers.

After a while Billy Joe reached up and scratched his unruly thatch of straw-colored hair. "How's things comin' on the place?" he ventured.

"Same as always," Troy grunted. "Stinks."

Billy Joe shot a glance at Troy's profile. The jaw was still thrust out in that old familiar, belligerent way. He knew when Troy had started that drumming on the counter with his thick fingernails that there was things comin' to a boil in Troy's mind.

"You sure don't like farmin', do you?" Billy Joe asked.

"I hate the sonofabitch!" Troy rasped.

Billy Joe retreated into silence again. He examined his chewed nails carefully. He sure as hell had to stop bitin' them; they were almost down to the quick. The thought of the farm persisted. "I sure as hell miss our place," he offered slowly. "I ain't much for livin' in town here."

"You got no bitch," Troy observed. "You got a good job, you come and go like you want. What the hell else is there?"

"It ain't the same."

Billy Joe knew the symptoms. He chose a long silence again. After a lengthy silence he spoke again. "What you doin' tonight?"

Troy roused himself and rubbed his palm over his forehead cautiously. "Reckon I might ride out by Nancy's. Maybe help her with her math or somethin'."

"You been doin' that a lot," Billy Joe remarked. "Helpin' her with her math."

"I like doin' stuff like that," Troy countered evenly.

Billy Joe sighed heavily. "Me and book stuff is strangers," he confessed mournfully.

Troy said nothing. It was true. He liked doin' the math problems; it came easy to him, gave him a kind of thrill workin' things out. Every now and then he came to town and helped Nancy with her work. Math wasn't one of her strong points. But, then, why should it be? Girls didn't need math; all they needed to know was taking care of the house, cooking, taking care of babies. Girls like Nancy, that is. Maybe, shorthand and typing were good, in case something happened and they had to help out at home. But something like math was a man's study and he liked it fine.

Billy Joe got to his feet. "I'm goin' over to see the movie. Sure you don't want to come see it, it's Pat Boone."

"Boone don't do nothin' for me," Troy sniffed. "Sounds like all the others."

"I don't know, he's got a kinda nice voice ..." Billy Joe trailed limply.

Troy was getting to his feet stiffly. His mouth contorted sharply as his weight sent a lightning jag of pain up his legs.

"Tom sure must have belted you good," Billy Joe commented with a kind of awed tone.

"Just stiff," Troy grunted.

Billy Joe held his peace. He'd have given his right eye to know what it was all about, but he'd learned a long time ago, if you were wise you didn't go horsing around too far with Troy where the family was concerned. If he wanted to tell you anything, he told it. If he didn't, well, forget it.

They stood for a moment outside the corner doors of the drugstore. Across the street the awnings in front of the hotel flapped in the biting wind from the north. On their right, the stark, stripped limbs of the trees on the courthouse lawn weaved and trembled, casting grotesque patterns on the light façade of the big square building behind them.

"I'll sure be damned glad when summer comes." Billy Joe shivered.

"Yeah, me too."

Billy Joe's eyes were on the marquee of the theater down the block. "Well, I'll be shovin'."

"Be seein' you, kid."

Billy Joe took a step or two, then turned again. "You and Nancy goin' skatin' Saturday?"

"Reckon."

"See you then." Billy Joe smiled faintly. "So long, Troy boy, keep your nose clean."

Troy grinned. "Keep your zipper up, pal."

As Troy bent forward to put the key in the ignition switch, he thought of Saturday. He drove with one hand holding the wheel steady, the other lying limply in his lap. Now and then, as he thought of Nancy, of the Saturdays yet to come, he reached down and touched himself, encouraging the warm, pulsing glow that had come to his loins.

# CHAPTER EIGHT

Ma closed the pages of her magazine with a sigh. She took off her glasses and raised a hand, rubbing at her eyes. Her words, when they came, were tentative, reaching out across the room like feelers. "They ain't nothin' wrong between you and Tom, is there, Cressy?"

Cressy's eyes widened. "Why, no, Ma ... no, nothin'."

The old lady shrugged and examined a fresh break in her nails. "He ain't been in the house all evenin'."

"Oh." Cressy glanced furtively toward the hall doorway. "He said somethin' about finishin' up on the tractor, Ma, somethin' like that."

"'Pears to me it's kinda late to be workin' outside this weather."

"Yeah ... yeah, it is," Cressy agreed miserably.

Ma eyed her with the quiet eyes. "What is it, Cressy?"

Cressy stretched her legs, made a cathedral out of her peaked fingers. "It ain't nothin' between us, Ma. You know him and Troy had an argument over somethin' this afternoon. It got him kinda upset, that's all."

Ma nodded. The trouble lines came home to her brow and she stared at the masking net of the lace window curtains across the room. "They always been scrappers, them two," she admitted slowly. "Tom, he's the solid one. He's like his Pa in that respect; he's easy-goin' and kind and thoughtful. He loves the land and he's a hard worker. Add to that he's got common sense and, as him and you get to buildin' your family here, long after Pa and me's gone on, he'll be makin' a good life for himself, for you and all the young 'uns. Troy?" Ma wet her lips and blinked. "He's a good boy and he's a right smart boy; he can go far, far away from here and far in his life, if he's a mind to. Yet, sometimes I don't quite rightly know what to make of that boy. Him bein' the youngest, I reckon I was always thinkin' of him as the boy-child, only I know he ain't that no more. He stands there in front of me and my eyes sees the bigness of him, the man-body of him. There's a kind of somethin', a kind of somethin' … I don't know …" She splayed her hands helplessly. "I know he ain't a bad boy! I know he's got the seeds of goodness in him, like Tom. I know he ain't even real wild, just young yet, and heedless and full of the hungerin' of the flesh and all. I get the feelin' he's kinda standin' at the crossroads, goin' right or maybe even goin' the other way, and it's somethin' I wisht I could help him with, only I can't. It calls up a kind of fear somewheres in me."

Cressy stared at her mother-in-law. Here it was, from the mother's lips herself, the confession that she, too, felt that something that seemed to be generating down inside Troy, that seemed to come flowing out from him, calling up the fear in all of them. Fear of what?

"What are you scared of, Ma?" Cressy leaned forward, her words soft, almost a hiss in the stillness of the room. "What's the thing in Troy really scares you?"

Ma's disturbed eyes rose and fixed intently on the taut face of the woman across from her. "I can't say," she shook her head slowly, "I can't say."

She got to her feet clumsily, achieved her balance and began gathering up the papers and the magazines, setting them in a neat pile on the floor beside the overflowing stand by Will's chair. Cressy made no comment, made no move to rise.

"You comin' to bed soon, honey?" Ma asked.

"In a few minutes, Ma. I'd kinda like a cigarette first."

"Shouldn't be smokin' them things right before goin' to bed," Ma reproved. "Ain't no good for a body." She moved toward the door. "I'm sayin' good night," she said to Cressy formally and turned and went off down the hall.

Cressy lit the cigarette and leaned her head on the old chair back. She closed her eyes to the brown stains that darkened the ceiling in spots, welted on the buckling paper like fungus growths. She smoked lazily. The old house seemed to be sighing, creaking, settling in for the night. From the far end of the house Cressy could hear the sounds of the parent couple preparing for bed.

Her mind wandered back over the things Ma had been saying. Troy had been fifteen that summer Tom had brought her home from Dallas. He'd been a big kid, even then, she remembered, standing a head or more over her. There hadn't been any wondering then. Troy had taken to her at first because she was his brother's wife, a kind of new curiosity. She had known that he had been watching her covertly under the shadow of his brows, speculating, making up his mind. He hadn't been around much then anyway, had been going to high school, going off with his buddy, that Billy Joe Everett.

All the troublesome stuff started when he got out of school, a big shot, who had come to flower during the two years he'd been home, working with Tom on the place, saving whatever he could, waiting until he could get down to Austin and the University. Then the restlessness and the woman-chasing and all the rest of it had begun to grow, the conflict between Tom and him, between the parents and him ... even between her and him; that's how it had begun and the waiting around was making it loom large and fearful. This was the thing that Ma felt, that Pa knew, that she and Tom discussed and worried about.

Cressy got up and crossed over to the ash tray, hesitated and went to the front door and opened it. The cold wind caught her up in a chilling embrace and she hastily snapped the cigarette end out into the yard and pulled the door shut again. Turning, she glanced around the room, crossed to the hall and switched off the light. Only the thin pencil-stripe of light under the far bedroom door broke the darkness of the passage.

Even though she knew every inch of the way, she guided herself cautiously, using the uneven bareness of the wall as her monitor. She paused just outside the door to the room she and Tom shared at the end of the house.

She reached down and released the catch and shoved the door a little. The half-light from the moonlit window shafted across the narrow room and touched the flat, empty bed. She frowned. Tom was not here; he must be up and about somewhere.

She turned away uncertainly, her hand still on the knob. It was getting late; by this time the whole household, with the exception of Troy, was generally in bed and fast asleep. Treading lightly she came down the hall to the kitchen. Stealthily she crossed over to the back door and moved quietly out to the porch.

The wind from the north had failed in strength. Only the little furtive whispers of the breezes eddied around her as she stood alone on the naked unsheltered landing and surveyed the barren yard.

There was no sound, no sign of him around the place. Perplexed, she moved down the steps and walked slowly across the crust of the wintry yard toward the black, rearing silhouette of the old barn.

At the small door she paused. She turned and glanced out toward the paved highway. Far off down along the fields there was a glow that widened and then sharply condensed into the twin points of headlights as a lone car raced along the lonely road to town. She waited until it had whined past the place. Then she drew a sharp, deep breath and forced open the little door.

Her eyes went to the soft yellowish glow of the lamp on the workbench and Tom sitting on the upturned crate, hunched forward, thoughtfully drawing little patterns in the slough covering the earthen floor.

Cressy made no sound. Hunched forward like that, alone in the flickering glow of the lamp, he looked so lonely, so pathetic, so abandoned. Quickly she came forward, moving across the shadowed floor, skirting past the dark hulk of the tractor until she stopped in the circle of light.

"Tom?" She hesitated. "Tom? What is it? What's the matter? It's gettin' so late, I been worried about you!"

For a moment she was shocked when he raised his head and stared up at her. The bruises on his cheeks were livid in the half-light, their fierceness heightened by the pale cast of his flesh.

"It's nothin'. I'm all right," he responded dully.

"It's time for bed, Tom."

"I—I just been sittin' here, just thinkin'." He stirred and tossed the bit of stick off into the swallowing shadow.

Cressy came forward swiftly. She dropped to her knees at his side and took his hands in hers. "Honey," she crooned, "don't let what happened today upset you so. It was just one of those things, just a brothers' fight, it's happened before, you told me so."

"It wasn't just today," he said, looking quietly down on her, "it wasn't just the fight."

Cressy tightened her grip on his hands. "Then what?"

"I don't know." His voice trailed off. He shoved himself to his feet, pulling from her hold, and went off a little way, standing with his back to her, his big arms hanging help-lessly at his sides, staring off into the darkened recesses of the place.

Cressy laid an arm across the still warm top of the crate to support her body as she stayed where she was. "What is it you don't know, Tom?"

"I don't know," he repeated in that vacant, empty sort of way. He turned and glanced back at her. His eyes were cloudy and the corners of his mouth seemed to her to be suddenly lined, deep and long, as if they belonged to a man many years older than her husband. "I been thinkin' about somethin' Troy said before I hit him, tryin' to think it out, to find the answer."

Cressy boiled. "Troy's nothin' but an ignorant, cocky school-boy!" she exploded.

Tom turned and looked down at her. His hand had risen as if he wanted to stop her words. "No ... you know better than that. He's a man in lots of ways. You see, he's got a brain and some-times that brain of his sees things kind of naked and in their proper place."

"All he ever thinks about is good times and women," she retorted bitterly.

"Yeah, I know. Most times, I reckon you're right." His voice went soft. "Only there's more goin' on sometimes in his head than anybody thinks."

"Such as?"

Tom took a long time to get underway. He was glad she had come to him, glad they were together now in the isolation of the old barn, glad they could talk together freely without the oth-ers around to interfere. Looking down on her, sitting like that, her eyes puzzled on him, her lips faintly parted, waiting, he remembered again the offhand, flippant comment of Troy's and wondered.

"I don't know how it all started," Tom began slowly. "We got talkin' about the place, about the land and all."

She nodded. "He don't like the land," she commented flatly.

"No, no ... he don't. He hates the place and everything that goes with it, to hear him tell it." He paused. "There's something else, too. He kinda puts the place and what happened to Pa together somehow. Somehow the place has put a fear in him about somethin' like that happenin' again sometime."

Cressy said nothing. She remembered suddenly how Troy had looked standing in front of his mirror, straight and tall, beautiful, no blemishes, no imperfections, flat-bellied and young male. "I reckon it's natural," she said slowly, "I guess most of us have a horror of bein' hurt or crippled in some way, like Pa."

Tom's voice grew distant. He raised his head, sent his gaze off into the darkness. "I remember how it happened with Pa. After Pa got sick like that, I don't know how we got by them first years. Somehow we managed. People was good. They helped out and we had enough to keep goin'. 'Course, by the time a couple of years went by, I started doin' more. By the time I was fifteen I reckon I was doin' most of it, with some help now and then, of course." He hesitated. "I reckon I never knowed any other kind of life, other than what I got."

"But you got it born in you, Tom. It wasn't like it is now with Troy!"

He glanced down at her and his eyes remained thoughtful. "Yeah, I reckon as how you're right there." He cleared his throat. "I wanted the land and it wanted me, so now I ain't got no complaints."

He fell into silence, a long silence, bringing his palms up from his knees and sitting there hunched over, staring down into the calloused cup of his hands.

Cressy slowly got to her feet. She walked idly along the length of the disemboweled tractor, tracing along the cool metal with the tip of her fingernail. At the end of the machine she turned and looked back to where he was. There was something more that needed saying, she knew that. In a moment she ventured her question.

"Then what started the brawl, Tom?" she asked quietly.

Tom's lips tightened and he again set his hands on his legs. He turned his head so that his eyes were on her and there was a kind of an uneasiness in them. "He said maybe, if somethin' like what happened to Pa ever happened to me, you might ... well, you might take off."

She caught her breath sharply. She came forward a step and wet her lips. "What makes you say a crazy thing like that?" she demanded, her eyes wide and angry. "You got no right thinkin' things like that, Tom, it's like borrowin' trouble when you start thinkin' things like that!"

"It could happen, it happened before," he said doggedly. He got up suddenly, came across the distance between them, put his big hands on her shoulders. He felt the stiffening in her body. "Troy said once anything like that happened to me, you'd blow the place, take off, head back to Dallas, maybe."

There was a long, injured silence. Her body under his steady, pressureless touch trembled faintly.

"You ought to know better than to go listenin' to a punk kid!" she snapped. "I give you credit for a little more common sense than that, Tom Bannock!" She stepped back and eyed him with angry reproach. "Since when does a man go listenin' to a boy?"

She moved past him angrily, almost throwing him off balance and went over to the box where he had been sitting. For a long moment she remained ramrod straight, silent, as if she were gathering her stormy thoughts, trying to translate them into proper words. When she turned to look back at him she was calmer, ready.

"Tom," she said quietly, "you remember back when we first met down there in Dallas?"

He nodded glumly. Almost abashed his eyes held her in their wavering glance.

"Remember where it was we met? We met in a bar, a beer joint, right there on the main drag. You remember what I told you then, when you bought me a beer? How I was different from you, how I been dancin' around in honky-tonkin' joints all over, goin' nowhere, how I just lost my job when that last place did an el foldo right there and I got stranded?"

He nodded. "I remember."

"Okay. Then you'll remember how I didn't mind at all when you took me for somethin' to eat and all. I was hungry, dammit, and if you'd done like the rest you'd have tried goin' on from there, tried to get me in some hotel room and collect for the meal and the free beer."

His face twisted sharply and his hand flew out toward her, as if he might sever the threads of her speech.

"No, hear me out, Tom. Okay. You didn't try. You just fed me and let me go. At first I must admit I was surprised. I figured you for a rhubarb, a big dumb joe from the country, was kinda pleased with myself for a smart one, figured you might even be good for a stake, see? I could maybe play you along and maybe I'd be able to clip you for the cash to get the hell outta Texas and back to civilization where I belonged."

He had half turned now and she faltered to a pause. There was a droop to his thick shoulders and suddenly everything in her wanted to go running across the little space between them. She wanted to throw her arms around him, pull him tight and close to her, to try and shield him from more hurt. She closed her eyes and plowed on with what she had to say.

"You fooled me, Tom," she went on softly. "By the time I could maybe have knocked you over for the stake, I found out I didn't want to get the hell outta Texas any more. I didn't want to go anywhere, do anything, if it wasn't goin' and doin' with you." She paused and took a deep breath. "Tom, that's what happened down there in Dallas. I found a man, not a boy, a man. It didn't matter if it was gonna be Texas or Timbuctu, I'd found what I guess I'd been lookin' for all along."

He turned now, his face bright with the new relief. She stayed him with the motion of her hand.

"I'm here now, Tom. Dallas is all gone and disappeared. Like last week's sand storm, it's all blown over. I'm Mrs. Tom Bannock, Cressy Bannock, and I live on the Bannock place. There ain't no way of changin' it, even if it might get rough sometimes, somehow." She took a step closer to him. "Your Ma knew that a long time ago when she and Will Bannock came out here and fought their way through thick and thin. Your Ma's a smart woman, Tom, don't ever sell her short. You think it made any difference to her, when your Pa got knocked out of action? Well, nobody knows, only I don't think it mattered a whoop in hell, bad as it was and bad as it's gonna keep on bein'. Nothin' mattered to her, so long as he's there at her side. She just had to do a little more, work a little harder ... only, it didn't change nothin' inside for either of 'em."

She quieted slowly. Now she stood silent, her eyes on the ground between them, following the half-obliterated traces of Tom's stick trail in the dust.

"And that's how it is, Tom," she added finally. She raised her head and her eyes widened in surprise. "You mean, that's how the ruckus started this afternoon? You two hittin' each other over whether I'd run off or not if there was trouble come?" The tears came to her eyes and she went to him. "Oh, you silly damn fool, you. You couldn't get rid of me with dynamite!"

Her arms went around his neck and she clung to him, drawing her breath in short, shuddering gasps, taking into her lungs the smell of his sweat, of his maleness. Tom Bannock reached down and caught her legs, swung her up easily and carried her over to the bench. Still holding her, he leaned down and blew out the little flame and, in the familiar darkness made his way carefully across to the half-opened little door. Outside in the stinging breeze that hinted of springtime, he nudged the door shut with his heel and started across the yard to the house.

# CHAPTER NINE

The sound of running water in the bathroom brought Troy's eyes open Saturday morning. Slowly his wits came alive to the day and there was a tingling in his limbs. Of all the days of the week Saturday was the best. It was the end, the most, the coolest. And this day, especially, was something worth getting up for!

There was the sudden hard rap on the closed door and the sound of his mother's voice. "Breakfast's nearly ready, Troy. Time you was gettin' a hump on!"

"Comin', I'm comin'!" he grunted.

Tom. His mind went to Tom. Tom hadn't said a word all day yesterday out in the field, working on the post holes. They'd worked together, like they always did, a team, working, easily, surely. Tom did the heavy work; Troy hung around, handing him the things he needed, lending a hand. Aside from asking for whatever he needed, Tom had said little. He had made no comment about the brawl the day before, had said nothing at all. Last night at supper nobody said anything. Nobody seemed to pay any attention to the bruises and cuts that had swollen and colored on both their faces. It was as if Pa and Ma and Cressy hadn't even noticed!

"Troy? You best be stirrin' in there. I'm not callin' again!"

Ma's voice snapped him to action. He darted across the hall to the deserted bathroom, dashed cold drops of water on his face, ran his hand over the spiked hair and headed for the kitchen, buttoning his fly on the run.

The three of them, Pa and Cressy and Tom, glanced up at him without expression as he came to a pause in the kitchen doorway. Ma, her back to him, worked at the stove, speaking without turning.

"Sit down, son, sit down. This here food's ready for eatin'."

Troy slid into place. Pa's eyes rested on him thoughtfully. Troy watched Ma as she heaped the platter with eggs and bacon and brought it over to them. She smiled as she put the platter down and, reaching over, ran her hand over the small spikes of his close-cut hair, in a rare, unfamiliar gesture for her.

"You're lookin' better this mornin', son," she commented. "Good night's sleep never hurt no one. You could be doin' with more sleep now and then."

Will glanced across the table at his youngest son, peering from the safe retreat of his heavy brows. "You boys finish up them post holes?"

Tom answered without looking up from his plate, "Couple of more left, Pa. I'll get 'em this mornin'."

Ma turned from the stove. "Now don't you-all go high-tailin' off in the field this mornin'. If we're goin' to town I want to get an early start. There's lots I want to do and I don't want to be draggin' in late."

"Won't take more'n an hour, Ma, you won't even be ready in an hour."

"Well … I just don't want to be gettin' in there after everything's been picked and hauled over."

"I was thinkin'," Cressy began guardedly, her eyes seeking out her husband across the table, "after the shoppin' and all's done, maybe we'd be able to see a movie or somethin'."

Ma stood half turned at the stove. "Might could do that, Cressy. Land sakes, I ain't been to the picture show in a long time now."

Will grunted. "Never did see much sense wastin' good time settin' in a dark room full of squealin' babies lookin' at a pack of ... make-believe!"

"Once in a while never did hurt nobody, Will," Ma protested sharply as she worked steadily, cleaning off the face of the stove, poking the wiping rag around the grease-splattered burner forks. It was only after Troy had shoved back his chair, had gotten to his feet, that she turned suddenly. Her words caught him in the hall doorway. "Troy? You're goin' in town with us today, ain't you?"

He shifted, scuffing his bare feet on the boards. "If you want, Ma."

"I want," she said flatly. Her eyes traveled down the frame of him, took in the old faded levis with the whitened fly and the worn areas on the thighs. "You're gettin' some new pants to wear around here," she stated firmly.

"Aw, Ma ... these are okay. Just like I like 'em."

"Hush your mouth now," Ma blocked him. "I declare to goodness, I never been so mortified in all my life as when you come inside yesterday through the front door and with Martha Dovely here, too. Them pants stickin' to your bones like that! It's a disgrace and I ain't gonna have it no more. You got one good pair for town and you're gonna get you another, so's you'll be decent around this house!"

Troy shrugged. His eyes traveled to the table but none of the other three were paying any attention to him and Ma and their private war. His gaze came to rest on his brother's bent head and he felt the sudden urge to say he was sorry for the other day, that he hadn't really meant all that crap. Only this wasn't the time or the place, not in front of the others like this.

"I'll be waitin' at the barn," he announced quietly.

"No need," Tom said, raising his head, meeting his brother's gaze. "What's to be done, I can do okay alone."

"I ain't got nothin' to do till we're ready." Troy's tone carried a shaded pleading.

Tom's gaze held level. There was nothing that Troy could see in his look, no resentment, no anger, no indication of anything at all.

"If you're so all-fired ambitious this mornin', you can clean up 'round that lousy tractor while I'm gettin' them holes. Set the tools and stuff up on the bench, straighten things up."

"Okay," Troy nodded meekly, "I'll clean up."

The four of them were silent after Troy left. It was Will Bannock who broke the spell surprisingly.

"He ain't willful, Tom," he observed quietly. "It's just he's plumb bustin' out with spirit. It was real thoughtful of him, offerin' to help out. He ain't much of a one to be willin'."

"He's okay, Pa," Tom grunted. "There's just times he gets on my tail, I reckon."

"It's always like that with brothers." Ma smiled warmly. "Been that way, I reckon, since time began. Law, I'm mindful how it was with my brothers, when they was young. Fightin' and scrappin' over every single thing until they was all married and fathers and settled down."

The eyes of Cressy and Tom Banock had come to a meeting. In them was knowledge and understanding, concealed and steady.

It was quite warm in town. The previous week's cold snap had broken and the early spring sunshine warmed the wide streets and bathed the shops and buildings with brightness. The white, boxlike modern courthouse, standing in the square, gleamed with clean-washed shine, and in front of the building the lawn showed signs of greening through the drab, straw slumber of winter. The tall trees had yet to put on their budding; their angular limbs were naked and raw, stretching up as if beseeching heaven itself for color. At the base of the trees the familiar squirrels had reappeared, busy on the dull grass, foraging out the bits and pieces of food.

Spring had made itself felt on the east end of town, too. There the Mexican farm workers thronged the sidewalks, clustered in knots in front of the Spanish-language theater, squatted in couples and family groups on the steps of the post office, sat around the old courthouse in their cars.

On the benches in front of the courthouse lawn, the old men reappeared, sitting around in old work clothes, whittling on their sticks, reminiscing old times.

West of the square the sidewalks carried their full weight of out-of-towners, the men in levis and freshly-washed overalls and khakis, tired men, with weather-lined faces and the West Texas squint-eyed look, eyes that had been pinched and held small against the glare and the wind and the sand of the open country.

Their women on the whole were simply women, ungirdled, their bellies big from hearty eating and rapid childbearing, their ample frames covered with shapeless cotton dresses, their feet large and comfortable in flats, their ears uniformly bedecked with overlarge, incongruous earrings and here and there a head grotesque in metal curlers.

In and around the parent couples were the kids, casually washed, casually brushed, casually dressed, boys and girls alike in the blue jeans that cost little and served all purposes.

Constantly there was a circling of automobiles. They came from the west end of town, fought their way through the two-block traffic jam in the downtown center, honking, spurting their wheels at stop lights, wandering without purpose. At the intersection they met the string of cars coming up the avenue from the north, cars filled with families, with teen-agers, with students from the college, with the out-of-towners. They made the turn into Broadway, headed west for a block, swung down the next street and skirted past the theaters and the hotel to make the run to the turn that would take them past the big drugstore and up the avenue to start the whole aimless circling all over again.

Troy stood alone on the corner across from the courthouse square. He peered closely at the parked cars near by. There was no sign of any of them yet. This is where they said to meet. Be there at four o'clock, Troy, now be sure, Ma had said. He sighed. The bulk of the new levis under his arm was an annoyance. His skin seemed to itch and he sneezed suddenly.

He turned and glanced up the far reach of the wide street. Off in the distance, out west, backgrounding the faint outline of the college buildings, he could already see the flung smear of color against the blue of the sky. There was no form to the tan wash, no outline; it seemed to blend, rather, into the sky's own color, to come spilling slowly, running as liquid might run when poured across a cloth. He sneezed again. The wind had come up gradually from the west. It came prodding, poking bits and pieces of paper along the gutters, sending them skittering nervously across the wide-bricked surface of the street, bringing the first dry, pore-clogging hint of the sandstorm to come.

Troy frowned and peered once more across the street. It was fifteen to four already. He hoped to hell they'd get there before the sand really started to fly. Somewhere a horn sounded close by, startling him. The horn blasted again, almost alongside him, and he raised hot, angry eyes. "For God's sake, shut up!" he bellowed into the pelting wind.

"Stop that yellin' and get in the car, quick now!" Ma commanded. Tom had brought the car up close to the curb, the door hung open and Ma worked to move herself over against Tom, making room for Troy. Pa and Cressy sat in the back, bundles heaped between them.

Inside the car, with the windows all rolled up, there was peace and shelter. Dust streaked across the black hood and there was a thick film over the dashboard already.

"Damn sand sure come up quick!" Troy said breathlessly. "Sure glad you come by when you did. I was like to be stung to death!"

"No matter how long I live I never get used to it," Tom grunted, concentrating on his driving.

"I hate it!" Cressy said from the back seat.

"Just have to put up with it," Ma observed quietly. "It's the Lord's doin'."

"Need rain, need rain bad, lots of it," Will commented. "That could be the Lord's doin', too," he added, his eyes on the firm, unbending head of his wife in the seat ahead.

"More people'd take time to go to church on Sundays and do some real prayin', maybe we'd be gettin' the rain," Ma returned crisply, her eyes finding her husband's face in the rear-view mirror.

"You get a chance to get to the show?" Troy glanced at his mother.

"No," she said sadly, "there just wasn't enough time."

"We could go now," Cressy hastened. "It's only four. We'd be out by six."

The trip to town wasn't complete without the movie. Ma's eyes found the mirror again and her mouth pursed dubiously. "You want to, Will?" she asked hopefully.

He was staring out of the window up the rows upon rows of used cars in the lots. "I reckon not. I'm gettin' kinda tuckered. Best I get on home.

"Yes … well …" Ma subsided.

Troy could almost feel his mother's let-down right through his body. He put his hand on her thick leg suddenly. "Ma?"

She twisted awkwardly and glanced at him, at the package in his lap. "I see you didn't lose them pants," she remarked.

"Ma, I'll take Pa on home. You-all go on to the show."

"No … no, that's not right."

"Why not, Ma?" Tom spoke up. "He could. After all, he's got his car. We'll drop him and Pa off, go on to the movie and be home in time for supper."

"No, Pa's tired out now."

"Well, he'll be home, Ma. He don't mind … do you, Pa?"

The old man was staring straight ahead, almost as if he had not paid any attention to what they were saying. His eyes were on the smooth back of his youngest son's neck, on the close-cropped glint of the blond hair where it trailed a shade more darkly brown into the concealment in the low collar. He had heard them. "Reckon that'll be fine with me," he said. "Anyways I get home's all right with me. Troy drives real good. I'd kind of enjoy ridin' home with Troy." He chuckled lightly. "Don't reckon as how I get much chance to go ridin' in one of these here hot-rod cars anyway."

"It ain't no hot-rod, Pa," Troy protested. "It's just been tinkered with, that's all."

"One thing," Cressy said grimly, "they'll sure know when you're comin', Pa."

"Well, I don't know …" Ma's eyes were uneasy on Pa in the glass above her eyes. She never felt quite right, taking off to enjoy herself on something that wasn't absolutely necessary, leaving him high and dry to fend for himself, even for a little while. It just didn't seem right, somehow, seemed to her to be stealing, like.

"Now, Ma, you just go ahead and see the picture show. Troy and me, why we'll get along fine." The old man coughed as a gust of wind hit the side of the car, spewing a pinch of the fine, powdery dust off the car window ledges.

Tom had brought the car up close to the parked black coupe. He got out without a word and went around to the back, coming up to open the door. There was the usual period of tussling, of twisting and turning, of grunting and easing before Will Bannock could manage to get safe on his feet on the street. He swayed unsteadily in the pummeling of the wind, held fast by his son's firm arms.

Troy slid out, left the door open and ran from the larger car to open the door of his own machine.

Will coughed again and blinked in the swirl of the dust and nodded toward the twin jutting exhaust pipes of the car. "Looks like one of them Vanguard things you read about," he chuckled. "Maybe we're goin' to the moon!"

Troy came forward and together he and Tom managed to ease their father into the car seat.

Tom shot a quick look at his brother. "You take it easy now, hear? Remember, Pa gets jumpy ridin'."

"Aw, screw you!" Troy muttered. "Hell, I know more about drivin' than you'll ever know, Jack! You think I'm just learnin' or somethin'?"

"Could be, the way you barrel-ass around town sometimes." Tom's jaw jutted and the flames in his eyes leaped. "There still some things you gotta learn yet, punk!"

Troy glared in the pin-pricking dust as his brother went to the other car. He followed in a moment and, leaning in, touched his mother's arm lightly. "You don't worry none, Ma, have yourself a good time."

"You takin' supper with us?"

"Naw, I'm gonna get cleaned up and back to town. Me and Nancy's goin' skatin'."

"But, supper ..."

"Don't worry, Ma," he interrupted irritably. "I'll get me a bite at the drive-in." He softened a bit. "It'll be okay, Ma. You just have a good time."

Troy saw that she was not listening to him, that her troubled eyes were on the dim figure of his father in the car ahead. "Don't worry, Ma, I'll take care of him fine," he promised.

He slammed the door, coughed to clear his throat and wheeled, ran ahead, opening his own door quickly, sliding on to the seat beside his father. The other car spurted and pulled away slowly, and, for a moment, Troy could see Cressy's face as she glanced through the back window at them.

"We need rain." The old man nodded, his eyes on the obscured top of the tall insurance building. "We need lots of rain so's the top soil will stay put." A vagrant wave of loyalty surged up through the old farmer. "This here," he pronounced, "is blowin' straight in from New Mexico."

# CHAPTER TEN

Troy rolled the car up close to the side of the low, squat building and turned off the engine. He sat there for a moment eyeing the parking lot curiously. Though the sandstorm no longer blew, there were only a few cars this early on a Saturday night, guys and gals grabbing a Coke or something before heading off for the dances, the movies or whatever. In a short spell the trim car hop came alongside his window.

"Hello, Troy," she smiled.

He grinned. His eyes dropped in routine evaluation over the pulsing blouse, traced the firm young legs that were snug in the creased slacks. "Where's Rita?" he asked casually.

"Oh, her? This is her night off."

"Oh?" Troy picked the keys from the dash and pressed down on the door handle. "I'm gonna get me some supper quick inside," he said.

"Okey-dokey."

He watched as she went prancing away to the next customer. She was new; she was all right, Troy mused, might not hurt to get to know that one better.

Inside the restaurant he slid on to the stool at the counter and glanced around. Some kids from the high school were bunched in the corner, smoking and talking loudly. Otherwise he had the place to himself. The woman stood before him, pencil in hand, waiting.

"Hamburger, with a slice of onion on the side. Coffee."

He had nearly finished the hamburger, leaning forward to avoid slopping the grease on his clean shirt front and tie, when the soft plump of a body next to him brought his eyes up. "Hi-ya, keed!"

Troy nodded, his jaws full of food. Billy Joe Everett grinned. Troy ran his eyes down the other man, took in the loud jacket, the sharp slacks and the open-necked sport shirt. "You got a new jacket."

"How you like that, man, cool, eh?" Billy Joe was pleased and now he twisted back and forth on the revolving stool, preening.

" 'S all right, boy."

Saturday night garb, like a uniform. Sport coat, white shirt, sport shirt, tie, slacks, period. All week long most of them wore levis and anything else. No fuss, no sweat. Now his neck hurt, was raw. Ma's put too much starch in the collar; it's like to chew my neck through. He ran his fingers around the inside and grunted. "Goddam thing's gonna kill me!" he choked.

"I dig you, man," Billy Joe sympathized. "They'll strangle you. Someday I'm never gonna wear a collar and tie again and anybody who don't like it can kiss my ass on the courthouse square at high noon!"

"You goin' on to the rink?"

"Yeah, later on, I reckon."

"Got a date?"

An odd, secret kind of smile crept over Billy Joe's face. "Sure thing, I got me a date."

Troy set the cup down and frowned at him. There was something mighty suspicious about the way Billy Joe was actin'. "Why all the big routine? You takin' Jayne Mansfield or somethin'?"

"Not quite, ole buddy, not quite." The sly wrinkles edged around the corners of his eyes. "Almost as good, they tell me, almost as good."

"Well, ain't that just the nuts," Troy chirped. He shoved back off the stool and stood, hitching up his trousers. "I gotta get goin', gotta pick up Nance."

"You got it real heavy on that Nancy babe, ain't you?" Billy Joe asked curiously.

"Balls!" Troy snapped. He went on ahead, paid the check. Taking a toothpick from the container on the counter he made a few idle jabs with it while the woman counted out his change. Shoving the bit of wood to the side of his mouth, he scooped the change and turned.

Billy Joe held the big glass door open and followed Troy out into the cool night. As Troy turned toward his car Billy Joe's hand caught at his sleeve. "Come on over to my car, I got some-thin' for you."

"Me?"

Billy Joe had already started across the paved parking area. Troy followed, frowning slightly at the delay. At the door of the old sedan Billy Joe waited for him to catch up. "Got a jug here, if you want it."

"How'd you get it?" Troy brightened.

"Pony come back from Big Spring this mornin'. I had him get us a couple."

"Sure thing!" That was the trouble livin' out here in a dry area. You had a helluva time gettin' any when you wanted it. The bootleggers had it, sure, but you paid through the nose for stuff you didn't even know how it was made! The best way was to have somebody bring back some if he was going the hundred miles or so to a town that had package stores or something.

Billy Joe had opened the car door and now he took up the bottle wrapped in a loose paper sack. "Treat it gently, man, this here's life blood!"

"Man, I sure can use this tonight!" Troy breathed appreciatively. The pressure of the almost-empty wallet bothered him. "How much?'"

Billy Joe shrugged. "Two-fifty." He caught the concern on Troy's face. "Hell, you don't have to pay me now. Gimme it later."

Troy's fingers tightened on the neck of the bottle. "Next week all right?"

"Sure."

Billy Joe went around his car and stood by the door. "We'll be seein' you out there later, okay?"

"Yeah, we'll be along. And ... thanks." He waved the bottle.

"Okay, Troy boy, take it easy with that fire juice."

"Don't worry, I'll treat it like it was uranium."

Troy walked back to his own car thoughtfully. Near the door he almost collided with the pert little car hop. She noted the clasped parcel and her eyes sparkled mischievously.

"Gonna have yourself a ball, big boy?"

"You ain't got no idea, honey." Troy laughed. He reached inside the open window, wedging the bottle in place in the glove compartment. He laughed again as he crawled under the wheel. "This here's gonna be a real time!"

She stood back in the shadow of the overhung roof and watched him back the low black car away. There was a sudden spurt, a roar and he was gone. No matter what they said, that Troy Bannock was a handsome hunk of man. She sighed. She remembered the bottle in the paper sack and her eyes narrowed. Somebody was sure gonna catch hell tonight, probably that Rita everyone said he was chasing.

Nancy Collins wore the female uniform of the week around town, the fluffy, stiff bouffant skirts, filled out with petticoats, topped with blouse, steadied with the short socks and flats. On

Saturdays, when they went to the rink, she wore a plainer, serviceable skirt, one that didn't take up so much room, one that slipped easily over the second skirt, the brief, flaring little bit that left her legs bare and free for skating. She finished her dressing, smoothed down the skirt and glanced at herself in the dresser mirror. Everything was ready.

She reached down and lifted the dresser runner carefully. There, hidden away for her own private moments, was the well-thumbed cutting from the newspaper, the picture of Troy when he had been a senior on the school swimming team.

He stood, big and broad, his shoulders thick, his chest full, his narrow, hard hips covered with the thin, tight black trunks, the thighs full, the legs long and straight. She bent forward and narrowed her eyes. The reproduction in the paper had blurred the more detailed parts of the picture but she could supply the missing part with her imagination. With her brightly-colored nail she traced the round of his chest muscles, touched the shadow of his chest muscles, touched the tiny dot of his navel. Her hand suspended and her cheeks flamed.

She raised her hot eyes and stared at herself in the mirror. There was a brightness in her eyes, a flush in her face, her lips sparkled in the reflection of the lamp. Her breasts pulsed with rapid breathing and she was conscious of the pinpoint hurting at their tips.

Hastily, guiltily, she slid the clipping back to its secret place and stepped back from the dresser, running her hot, sweating palms down the sides of the rough skirt, taking away the stickiness, the sleekness from her fingers. At that moment she heard the striking of the door chime, the far-away tapping of her mother's heels on the hard wood of the hallway, the murmuring of distant voices downstairs.

"Nancy? Nancy girl? Troy's here!" her mother called.

She moved tremblingly toward the door, fighting to regain her strength, her composure. She opened the door and stood there and forced a swallow. "I'm coming," she called.

She waited a few moments, until it was safe, until the pressures had lessened a little, until her mind had come alive through the eddying smoke of her fantasy. Then, carefully, she moved out into the hall and came to the top of the stairs.

At the base of the steps her mother stood talking happily with Troy. He had his back to the stairs and Nancy looked down on his blond head, on the funny little whiteness of his scalp where the hairs had been clipped the shortest. Then, drawing herself tight and secure, she moistened her lips and started down to join him.

# CHAPTER ELEVEN

The first glance gave the place away. The Happy Times Roller Rink was cheap and garish. At the far end of the hall there was a kind of upraised stage where, now and then, programs were put on, an occasional western band of local vintage or a rock'n'roll combo would play for the crowd. This was done on "special" occasions. On a night such as this particular Saturday, there was no "live" entertainment. The music came spilling out loud and tinnily, blaring from a souped-up juke box.

From the ceiling hung soiled and ragged streamers, remnants of some gala evening now long forgotten. Around the edge of the arena there was a three-foot board fence, festooned with faded, crudely-painted ads for city business, and above this fence there were banked rows of hard wooden bleacher seats rising to the juncture of wall and ceiling.

The racket was constant and varied. It seemed to rise and fall, first high in volume and then low, as the skaters wheeled around the course. Now and then the mixture of grinding skate wheels on the worn floor boards and the raucous blare of the jazzy music was pierced by the sharp, excited screams of a girl and there would follow a burst of yelling and laughter from some group horsing around the floor.

At the entrance to the arena sat Harry Marvel, his hat shoved back to expose the faint traces of the red hair strands, cigar shoved to one corner of his mouth, stuck between those thick, full, sensuous lips. He sat with his chair tilted back, so that one well-worn boot was set against the short wall on the other side of the narrow entrance passage that led from the fitting room to the skating area.

He sat like that for hours, his eyes shelled, his gaze on the boiling mass on the floor, detached and disinterested, his body shifting only as he moved the leg barrier to let more skaters come and go from the floor. His thick hairy left arm lay asleep across the pressing bulge of his belly; his right passed beneath so that his big ham of a hand lay idle across his lower belly, the fingers dropped into the crevice between his heavy legs. Only now and then, in the fitful motion of abstraction, would the thick fingers twitch and Harry Marvel would vaguely scratch at his genitals.

This was Harry Marvel's kingdom, the Happy Times Roller Rink. It was Harry's private opinion that the goddam joint cramped his style. Still it was his, legal, all his. Like his woman, like that goddam Rita, it was all his.

Sometimes, when Harry got to thinking, sitting here like this night after night, for the whole ten years he'd been fronting the joint, it seemed like the same bunch of kids had been coming every night all that time. Sometimes, when he was looking at them and seeing them, he couldn't do it any more; he'd have to close his eyes or look away or else he'd be puking on the floor, just with having to look at the goddam little punks and their broads.

Harry sat now, trying not to look at them. He tried to think about Rita and her long, long legs, that belly and the breasts and the way she came to him, no matter what was written in her hot, wet eyes. He took the cigar from between his lips and eyed the butt with distaste, running his tongue around the inside of his mouth to try and wipe away the dirty taste. Grunting, he came forward on the chair, fumbled in his pants' pocket for the big kitchen match, tilted back and sucked in the flame; his eyes were blind to the sign overhead that he himself had painted, the one that said no smoking in the hall.

With a sniff he shoved the cigar back to its original place, set his big boot against the wall and went back to his musing. If it wasn't for the booze he peddled to the kids, by God he'd have hauled ass out of this dump and gone on back to Houston a long time ago, or some place where there was some life going on.

There was a pressure on his leg and Harry took the cigar from his lips and scowled. He peered up at the couple waiting to get to the floor and then his cigar went back and his leg came down. It was that cute little Collins broad and her boy friend, that big Troy Bannock.

"Hi-ya, kids." He smirked expansively. "Gonna have yourself some good clean fun?"

"We're gonna try," Troy said coolly.

Harry brought his eyes up slowly from the two little pear breasts almost in his face. For a moment his lips compressed into a straight line, barely rounding over the interference of the cigar. Troy Bannock was standing there, not coming inside the barrier, just standing, looking down on him as if he were eight feet tall or something.

Harry took his narrowed eyes from the insolence of the face above and let them slide down over the wide-shouldered sport coat, the white shirt and the long strong legs inside the neatly-tapered slacks. The little burning came along Harry's spine, and the fingers across his belly came together like meshing cogs.

As the couple pushed past him, going to the opening in the floor barrier, Harry licked his lips. Now there was a piece, nice and fresh, just asking for the taking. His eyes shifted again to the tall boy. Troy towered over her, his bigness made even more apparent by the contrast. Harry rolled his cigar with his tongue and sucked on the tip, his eyes on them through the smoke. He sure is one big sonofabitch, he was thinking; he wondered now, as the couple stepped out on the floor, if the bastard was getting any.

"Glad you came?" Troy asked Nancy.

She flushed and squeezed his hand. "I'm having a wonderful time," she answered almost shyly. "You're such a good skater, Troy."

He swelled and his shoulders moved back a little. "Hell, I been skatin' ever since I was a. kid."

"You know just what to do and when to do it," she admired. Her eyes were busying themselves identifying the others as they swung past them. There wasn't a couple on the floor with the style and the smoothness that she and Troy had and she knew it and gloried in it.

That stupid punk Marvel was sitting back on his big fat can, that hunk of beef of his propped up across the entrance, and he was watching them through the veil of smoke. Troy knew what the big slob was looking at; Harry Marvel had a reputation for getting his hands on the young ones, if he could. There had been that time not so long ago when he'd gotten caught out back of the place with his hand all the way up Betty Ann Garner's dress and Will McSorley had beat the living shit out of him, whipped him for sure, left him bawling his little pig eyes out in the dirt, so they said. Since then Harry Marvel kept his hands where they belonged; it was only his little dirty eyes that kept on working like before.

They skated on in silence, Troy with his arm easily around Nancy's slim waist, their strokes matching perfectly, so they didn't have to think at all, just go gliding along in time with the music, go 'round and 'round the rink floor with no effort at all.

The music crashed through to a finish and there was some scattered applause. Troy braked his skates and pulled Nancy around him, gathering her up close to him at the finish. He stood holding her close, and his eyes, over her shoulder, met those of Harry Marvel, and he saw the older man take that damn cigar from his mouth and just sit there, staring across the arena floor, just looking in an ugly sort of way.

Tightening his lips, Troy turned so they had their backs to him. They skated across the floor slowly to the small gateway in the barrier and clumped up the few steps to where her skirt was and sat down on the bleacher bench. He kept Nancy's hand in his, holding it close to his belly.

Nancy eyed him with excitement. "You look so nice tonight, Troy, all dressed up like that."

"Shucks." He blushed suddenly. "I ain't got nothin' on special, just the old sport coat and slacks you seen a hundred times before."

"I don't care, tonight you look real nice." Her hand worked its way so that she was clasping his fingers. "I'm real proud of you, Troy."

He felt an unaccustomed glow of pleasure. He suddenly bent down and kissed her gently behind the ear, in the place where the hairs were soft and downy, clean smelling in his nostrils. "I think you're the nuts," he whispered huskily.

Nancy's hand rose and she caught the back of his head, feeling the moist warmth of the smooth skin at the nape of his neck. She said nothing. Suddenly she became conscious of the time and the place and she pulled away, bringing her hand down, clasping both tight in her lap. "There's some of the kids coming in," she said.

Troy slipped his arm around her shoulder and they sat watching a group pressing past Harry Marvel to the floor. The joint was beginning to fill up now; there was an almost continual stream of skaters making the wide circle of the floor. In the open center two couples were jiving it up to the music, pounding against the battered floor boards with the steel skates in a weird jungle beat.

"You want to skate some?"

"No, not just now." She snuggled back against him. "Let's just watch."

Harry Marvel was watching, too. He watched the skaters and his mouth went ugly and his eyes receded in the beefy flesh of his red face. He'd told them goddam kids a hundred million times to knock off that jam-session stuff on the floor. Hell! They'd have the place driven down into the foundation if they didn't quit! From his shirt pocket he fished out the silver police whistle and blew lustily. The shrill blast pierced the din and scored a direct hit on the dancers. Instantly they stopped, all four throwing startled glances at the source of the blast; then they melted anonymously into the whirling mass of the moving skaters.

Harry replaced the whistle irritably. In ten minutes they'd be back out there, he knew, stamping the hell out of the place. Christ, keeping an eye on the bastards was like baby-sitting, you never knew what they were up to and they sure as hell were up to something every minute of every hour!

His little eyes drifted over the bobbing heads of the patrons to the bleachers beyond. He could see them now, her and that big bastard, sitting up there, all cozied up, all by themselves. One thing Harry knew, if it was him dating that chick he wouldn't be wasting no time sitting in no bleachers loving her up. He'd have her back down on some car seat, giving her as much as she wanted, as much as she could take!

"Get your goddam leg outta the way, Harry!"

Harry Marvel's thinking snapped back angrily and he stared up into Rita's grinning face. His flesh darkened under the boil within him. "What the hell you doin' here, Rita?"

Her grin was insolent and knowing. "Just come by to see you, hon," she purred.

Harry took the cigar from his lips, held it out before him like a dirk as he let his chair come forward. He sat hunched forward a little, his head twisted on his thick, bull neck, angled, his eyes small and hard on her. "I thought I told you to keep the hell away from here; I don't want you hangin' 'round the dump, you know that!"

Rita fluffed her long black hair back casually and drew back her shoulders. She wore no brassiere and the faint pointing of her nipples was plain beneath the sheer blouse. She shoved her hands down in the pockets of her slacks and balanced teeteringly on the high heels. "Just kinda got lonesome for you, hon," she pouted, "just had to see what my old baby was doin'."

As she spoke the hint of alcohol drifted down to Harry. "You been drinkin'!" he charged.

"Sure, I been drinkin'," she replied jauntily. "You sure don't think I'd be comin' 'round a joint like this if I didn't do no drinkin' first, now do you, Harry?"

"I don't like no drunks here," Harry growled.

"Come off it, Harry, for God's sake." She tried to focus her eyes on the swirl on the floor. "Looks like you got a real nice crowd, Harry."

He pushed back in his chair and eyed her coldly. He'd told her hundreds of times; don't come around the rink, he'd said, 'specially not when you got a heat on, he'd said, and she always wound up doing what she goddam well pleased. She brought the temper in him to a high boil. Someday, someday this broad was gonna do something an' he was gonna bash her, fix her can once and for all.

She was grinning down on him and she let her fingers brush across his shoulder. "Relax, hon, you never had no trouble with me when I been takin' on a few, now have you?"

Harry conceded reluctantly. It was almost true. Rita could hold her own. "Well, you better be watchin' it, you ..." He warned.

"Why watch it?" She shrugged. "It ain't gonna change, me watchin' it. You sure as hell ought to know that, Harry." She laughed lewdly.

He grinned suddenly. By God, Rita was somethin', all right. In the midst of the grin he noticed something. He came sitting bolt upright, his eyes sharpening on the guy right behind Rita. He hadn't moved since Rita had touched him, had just stood there dumbly behind her. The character was about six-foot-two, stringy, young, fresh off the cotton patch. He wore a pair of clean-pressed levis that hung from bony hips, covering long, thin legs, and he wore a faded denim jacket. His hair was a funny kind of blond, straw-colored and unruly. A real cornball from Corn Center, Harry thought contemptuously. God, what a rube! Slowly his head turned and his eyes fastened evilly on Rita. He carried the silent question to her with the flick of his head.

Rita flushed. Her laugh came a little too quickly. "I brought you a payin' customer, Harry. My cousin." She laughed again and the big lunk made the mistake of laughing, too, as he moved in a little closer to her.

"Out," Harry Marvel said once.

The guy stopped cold and looked helplessly from Harry Marvel's cold little eyes and the full, cruel mouth to the woman standing at his side now.

"Aw, Harry ... He just wants some fun ..."

Harry Marvel's eyes never left the paling face of the farm boy. "Out," he repeated icily.

Rita stared down at Harry. She knew that look; she'd seen it here, seen it on the streets, seen it in bed close up, and she knew what was behind it. Nervously now she turned to the kid and her lips trembled in an insecure smile. "Hon, maybe you best do like he says, maybe you best go …" She faltered. "Maybe it's best …"

"If this guy …" The farm boy made a threatening step forward.

Harry made no move. He sat rocklike, evil, ready. "Out," he repeated thickly.

"Hon … it's all right … you go … go!" Rita gave him a shove back the way they had come.

The farm boy stumbled, looked from one to the other in that helpless, bewildered way. Still wearing the look of consternation, he shrugged and turned away. In a moment he had disappeared through the fitting room toward the entrance to the building.

Harry's eyes were on Rita. His lips had thinned and there was no blood in them. "One of these here days," he promised distinctly, coldly, "I'm gonna catch you whorin' around and there's gonna be two dead 'uns, you and him. You don't forget it, hear?"

Rita made a vague, faint gesture with her hand. "It was just for kicks, Harry, you know that."

"You get your kicks from me. Anytime you want kicks you let Harry Marvel know. I got everything you're needin'."

Rita shifted uneasily. She glanced out over the floor, not knowing whether to go inside or turn back. Harry caught her indecision. "You go on inside. You ain't about to be goin' back that way, not for a while, you ain't."

Rita looked down at him and, for a second, her mouth tightened and there was a hardness in her eyes. What the hell right had he, ordering her life, as if everything she thought or did and breathed and all belonged to him alone, all of it owned by Harry Marvel. As the anger came washing through her insides, scalding along the walls of her belly, she wheeled from him and walked away, making her way unsteadily along the rim of the skating area, working to avoid the skaters, heading for the back of the place, where the toilets were, where the crowd was, where she could get away from him and his goddam eyes and his goddam mouth, for a few minutes anyway.

It wasn't until later in the evening that the place really began to jump. The skating grew faster and more unbridled and the sweat began to flow freely. There was hardly a number now that found Troy and Nancy sitting down. They had thrown themselves into the melee, getting a kind of mutual kick out of the mounting excitement of the swift-moving, ear-splitting activity.

Finally Nancy could take it no more. She tugged on Troy's sleeve and pointed to the side wall. In a moment they had disengaged themselves and glided into an open area.

"I'm beat," she panted. "Let's sit out for a while, please, Troy?"

"Sure thing." He helped her up the steps and they plopped gratefully into a seat. "Man," he grunted, swiping at his forehead with his handkerchief. "It's hot as hell when you get goin'."

"I know," she agreed. "I'm simply boiling!" She could feel the little sweat droplets skittering down, between her breasts, the dampness on her belly, back and loins. Uncomfortably she shifted, trying to ease herself.

"You want a Coke or somethin'?"

"Okay."

"You stay put; I'll be right back."

Troy clambered down the steps to the floor, skated along the fringe of the crowd toward the refreshment bar at the front of the place. His eyes were busy, skipping over the faces of the milling crowd, but there was no sign yet of Billy Joe.

He came to the floor exit, to the thick leg barrier attached to Harry Marvel. "Put it down," he said, motioning to the beef.

Harry Marvel eyed him with sharp distaste. He lowered the boom with a grunt. "You got yourself a nice little piece of quiff, friend," Harry observed with an oily voice.

"I know," Troy agreed, his face hardening. "And it's all mine, Marvel, all mine."

"You're a right lucky boy," Harry admired nastily. "You must be livin' right."

"That's what I reckon."

Harry Marvel sat on his haunches on the chair and watched the back of Troy Bannock as he went from him, as he was swallowed in the gathered crowd by the bar. Suddenly he took his cigar from his lips and eyed it. It had gone dead. He dropped it to the floor between his thick thighs and shoved himself from the chair. Walking lightly for one so heavy, he made his way along the curving rim of the barrier until he came to the opening to the bleacher steps. There he stopped and glanced up. She was there all right, sitting alone, watching the floor full of skaters. Harry's eyes sharpened on two slender legs, on the muscled thighs that were revealed at the hem of the little skating skirt. He moved quietly up the steps until he came to her side.

"Havin' fun?" he asked genially.

"Oh, yes, Mr. Marvel, it's lots of fun. I love to skate!"

"You skate good," Harry observed smoothly. "I been watchin' you out there. You ought to get in one of my contests sometime, you might could win."

Nancy blushed. She looked down at her hands in her lap and twisted her fingers in embarrassment. "Oh," she laughed self-consciously, "I'm not that good. I ... I'm just a skater, that's all."

"Well," Harry moistened his thick lips, letting his eyes feast on the blouse, on the tender young legs, "you're the best lookin' skater we got here tonight."

"Thank you," she said quietly.

"Yeah," Harry grunted. His eyes bugged on the two provocative little mounds almost concealed in the folds of the blouse.

"Hi, Nancy ..."

Her eyes fled from Harry Marvel's hungry face and she broke in a smile of relief. "Billy Joe! We been watching for you all night!"

Harry Marvel's face stiffened. He turned and stared at the younger man at his side.

"Hi, Mr. Marvel, you sure got a crowd here tonight!"

"Yeah. Lots of kids tonight," Harry parroted unevenly.

"Where's Troy, Nancy?"

"He's gone for Cokes; he'll be right back."

Billy Joe looked from Harry Marvel to Nancy and then back at Harry. In her eyes he had read the silent, pleading request. He grinned casually. "Reckon as how I'll hang 'round for the old boy, if you don't mind."

" 'Course not!"

She slid over a little and Billy Joe dropped down at her side, sitting up close to Harry Marvel's knees, between Nancy and the owner.

Harry said nothing more. He gave a kind of grunt and then went back down the steps ponderously, retracing his steps to his post at the entrance.

Neither Nancy nor Billy Joe made any comment as they watched his big hulk go. Finally Billy Joe shook his body, as if he were ridding himself of something clinging.

"I don't go much for that Marvel character," he observed sourly. "If you ask me, he's creepy."

Nancy's smile was thin. "Oh, he's all right, I guess. He's … Well, he's just older," she excused.

"Older, yeah." Billy Joe studied Nancy's profile as she watched the skaters down below. "Maybe that's it," he agreed slowly, "just 'cause he's an old bastard."

Harry Marvel had no sooner taken up his position again than his leg was tapped again. He glanced up with a scowl. Bannock had the waxed containers of Coke in his hands, stood waiting to pass.

"Havin' yourself a little party, eh?" his eyes rested on the containers. "You're short one, friend; some other guy's sittin' with your girl."

Troy's eyes rose to where she sat and he saw Billy Joe. "Don't worry none about it, dad," he replied crisply, "it's an old friend of the family."

Harry wet his lips. His eyes were still on the containers. "Need somethin' in there to kind of sweeten things up a bit? Somethin' maybe a little stronger? Hear tell it's good for relaxin' some muscles and puttin' the old pepper in the other."

"I never needed no juice yet," Troy sneered down on him. "When I do, I know where there's some and it won't be comin' out of that crummy stock of yours, Marvel."

"Smart boy," Harry nodded, the faint, humorless smile on his lips. "We got us a very smart boy."

"Damn smart," Troy snapped.

Back in the seat Troy handed Nancy her drink, offered his to Billy Joe and was refused. In a moment Billy Joe excused himself and left the two alone. Troy sat down and took a swallow. He curled his lips in distaste for the sweet stuff and a look of pained sufferance edged around his eyes. Maybe Marvel had somethin' at that! What this slop needed was a good jolt. He thought longingly of the pint stashed away in the glove compartment of the car. Sliding a long measuring glance at Nancy sitting there quietly, at peace, he took a breath. "I gotta go," he announced.

She grinned. "Like the man says, when you gotta go ..."

"You be all right?"

"Sure." She remembered Harry Marvel's intrusion the last time. "Only, Troy?" He was looking down on her now. "Hurry back?"

"You bet." He pressed her shoulder and clumped down the long aisle to the floor. He skated along slowly, the cup in his hand, working his way toward the rear of the building.

Inside the smelly men's room there were a couple of guys sneaking drinks, laughing, summing up their dates, according to specifications and records. Troy paid little attention. He relieved himself and then went out, emerging in the humid, noisy backwash of the hall, peering through the half-light, until he had found the open back door that fronted the parking lot. As he started forward there was the touch of a hand on his shoulder and he glanced back surprised into Rita's glowing eyes.

"Where the hell you off to in such a rush, big boy?"

"How ya doin', Rita?" His eyes had slipped down her, sliding to the deep cut in her blouse, to the shadowed crevice. "What the hell you doin' here?"

Rita shrugged and rolled her eyes. "Just killin' time before it kills me. Night off." Her interest picked up. "You alone?"

"No." Troy could feel his face grow hot. "I'm with somebody."

Rita's eyes softened a little. You couldn't help going for the big bastard, there's something so goddam clean and decent about him, real decent, no matter the horsing around. "The same one?" she needled gently.

"The same one."

"The little schoolgirl type."

"Yeah, I reckon you might could say that."

She measured him now against the half-light and remembered that night in the car by the abandoned old gin. "Wonder if she's got enough for you?" she murmured absently.

"You ... you want a quick drink, maybe?" He spoke impulsively.

The dry cottony taste was thick in Rita's mouth with the effects of the earlier drinks slipping away fast. "I sure could use a quick pickup," she agreed fervently.

"Come on, I got one in the car."

Together they went out into the night, Troy clumping along over the gravel on the skates, Rita mincing her way carefully on the precarious high heels, her fingertips on his forearm to steady herself. The wind was cold, stinging on their flesh.

At the car he opened the door and snapped down the lid on the compartment, bringing out the sacked bottle. Unscrewing the cap, he gave it to her. Her eyes as she took the parcel glinted in the light from the distant building.

"Here's how ... and how!" She laughed throatily. She tilted the bottle and helped herself to a generous succession of lusty swallows. As she took the bottle down her gaze fell on the lighted rectangle of the back door and she started sharply. There he was, Harry, the goddam, spying bastard, standing there, full-framed in the doorway, looking out over the parking area, not moving, just standing there looking.

"What's the matter? You sick?" Troy stared at her.

"Christ, no!" She forced her laugh and handed the bottle back to him, making a wry face and a circular motion with her hand on her belly. "I ain't been sick drinkin' since I was twelve. You think I'm the little schoolgirl type?" She wiped her lips with the back of her forearm. "That sure starts the old engines wor-kin'," she quipped. Her eyes moved restlessly and she sought out the lighted hole in the wall again. There was no one there now; he had turned and gone back inside. Rita breathed easier and her lip curled. Goddam know-it-all Harry bastard!

Troy took his drink. Like she said, it started things going, brought the deep exciting spiral through his belly, sent its mes-sage along his grapevine nerves. He offered her a second swig.

She took the bottle and this time limited her swallows, careful not to kill what was left.

When she had returned the bottle she leaned back against the car and stared up into the sky, brushing her hair back with her wrist. Troy finished the bottle and tossed it over the roofs of the near-by cars, listening fascinatedly until it hit on dirt and not on metal. His eyes came back to Rita. She was bent sharply back, her body strained, her long legs slightly spread, bracing herself, and her eyes were half closed.

"Feel better?" he asked thickly.

"Man, you bet I do," she breathed. "Like a new doll, almost." She widened her eyes on the sweep of the cloud-less, star-flecked sky. "It's so goddam clean out here, almost like it was spring already."

"You're spring out here," he said huskily.

He was standing almost directly in front of her, his eyes greedy on the spread of her lush body. Rita turned her head slightly and stared at him. There was too much of this one; she'd known it the other night, knew it now, knew it was not right, not even on her side of the fence. Too much body, too much good looks, too much decency, too much brains. She was happier, more comfortable in the long run sticking with some bastard like Harry Marvel, her own class, even with that stringy hayseed she'd picked up some-where earlier tonight. She didn't understand this Troy Bannock. With the others she knew where she stood, what it would be like, where it would end before it even got started. With this one, she lost her bearings somehow, got all fussed up.

His arm had slipped around her, his big hands coming up the reach of her back, taking her from the cool of the car side, bringing her hard against the wall of his chest. He had stepped in between her legs and now his head was bent, blocking out the sight of the stars, and his hard, firm tongue had forced between her teeth and was seeking out the warm hollow of her mouth. A little moan came from her as she tried to turn aside, to escape the hold of his tightening arms, his thrusting hips, his harsh painful grasp.

"Damn you!" She broke free suddenly, wrested from his clutch and spun away, bumping her body along the length of the car. She caught herself at the rear of the machine, clung to the tail fin and stared at him. "This ain't no place, for God's sake!" she rasped. Her sight fled back to the dark bulk of the building, to the warning, lighted opening eye at the back. "You get started like that, you can't stop!" she cried.

He stood unsteadily, right there where she had broken from him. His clothing was disarranged, his face shiny with sweat. For a moment he returned her stare, numbly, uncomprehendingly. It had all come on him so suddenly. All of a sudden it had been like being caught up in a giant wave that tumbled him bodily into a black, swirling evil pool. He fought to catch his breath, to stem the thing that brought a panic in its wake. Without a word he spun away on the skate wheels and went clumping off blindly between the cars, heading for the rink building, the lights and safety.

Inside the door, safe once again in the murky heat of the hall, he stumbled to a halt. He reached out and seized the door jamb and hung on. What had happened out there hadn't just been sex this time, not just that old feeling once more and the wanting and the heat of it. There had been something new, something strange, something terrible and fearful. It had been as if he had skidded right up to the brink of a yawning hole, a pit black and bottomless and full of horror.

Finally, when he felt he could, he gave his body a little shove and rolled forward to the edge of the skating area. Bringing his head up he searched the jam-packed hall. Harry Marvel was not in his place by the entrance slot; instead there was some kid, seated with his blue-jeaned leg in place, aping the owner's position. Raising his eyes he found Nancy where he had left her, sitting small and alone, huddled on the bleacher seat, her eyes now picking him out of the crowd, her hand lifting in recognition. Troy stood there alone, with the crowd swirling around him, and for the first time in his life he felt the unrest of wrong, the thick, dirty scum of shame in his mouth.

"Hey, Troy boy!" The greeting bounced from the floor ahead of him. Billy Joe Everett and that redhead looker he chased around with sometimes, Cora Sue Chalmers, flashed by, skating together, laughing and waving.

Troy waved absently. He felt tired all over. There was a straining ache in his back muscles and his legs felt leaden. He forced his feet to move, to call the skates into action. Slowly he drifted along the barrier, moving counter-clock-wise to the whirlpool, until he had come to the first of the steps up into the bleachers.

As he reached the seat tier and sank down beside her, Nancy leaned toward him and her hand covered his. If she was able to detect the smell of whisky, she said nothing about it. Instead she gave him a soft smile.

"All of a sudden I'm beat!" Troy mumbled. "I'm just plain pooped!"

She could feel now the hidden trembling in his body, the taut, coiled restraint. She felt him stiffen slightly, caught the quick, darting movement of his head and followed the sudden glance that had widened his eyes. That ugly Harry Marvel had come to the edge of the floor at the back of the rink and he was standing there, a little apart from the knot of the crowd. His hands were shoved deep in the back pockets of his trousers and he was looking up over the heads of the skaters at them. Nancy shivered slightly. There was something about Harry Marvel that brought the light lick of fear to her; there was something kind of hidden and wicked and reptilian in the mere way he held his body.

In a moment the wheeling skaters had bunched on the floor, had hidden him from their sight. She sneaked a side-long glance at Troy. He was sitting straight, his eyes still on the place where the rink owner had stood. He quivered and she saw him wet his lips gingerly. She tightened her clasp on his big hot hand. "Is there anything the matter, Troy?" she asked softly. "Is there anything wrong?"

He shook his head but said nothing. They just sat there, looking down. Slowly the tension began to lessen; she could feel him grow quieter and that tight look around his eyes was going.

"You want to skate some?" he finally asked.

She nodded. "Yes, let's."

He helped her to her feet and they went carefully down to the floor. Still not speaking they joined the moving crowd and made the big circle, skating just a little behind Billy Joe Everett and that Cora Sue Chalmers. They seemed to be having such a good time, Nancy reflected, so carefree and happy. Troy just skated on and on grimly, his arm around her waist, holding her close to him.

Nancy groped and found his hand against her waist. She pressed her palm against his fingers, feeling the strength of him. Somewhere deep inside her was that gentle, lapping disturbance, a feeling born without reason, without a name. There was a kind of hollowness come to her. She held her hand on his, as if through this contact she might bring him back from that unknown plateau to which he had fled. She had no knowledge of what it was that had brought this about, but, down deep inside her, she knew it was bound up somehow in that staring, level look that had been in Harry Marvel's eyes only minutes ago.

✤   ✤   ✤

As the time wore on, the confusion drifted slowly from Troy's mind. He became conscious of her hand on his, of her body under his clasping arm. He glanced down at her and saw that she was smiling up at him, her eyes wide and clear, her lips slightly parted, the bright lights overhead gleaming in prisms in the lacquer of her lipstick. He felt a sudden wave of pride come filling, seeping into the chinks and hollows of his being. She was the best-looking girl on the floor and he knew it! His arm tightened suddenly around her and brought a little squeal.

"Troy! You're cutting off my breath!" she gasped.

It was not a complaint; it was a welcome home. The fears and the puzzling in her had burst and evaporated in the instant.

"Let's show 'em really how to do it!" he cried exultantly. The juke box was pouring out rock'n'roll, mixing the blare with the grinding din of skate wheels on the floor boards. Troy expertly maneuvered her into place and began his steps. All their times of skating together paid off now and they skated easily, knowingly, fitting into a unity through experience.

Soon there was a little space cleared by the others as Troy and Nancy danced the quick steps, their skate wheels tapping out the rhythms on the boards. The widening circle stretched and soon they had most of the floor to themselves. Now they let themselves go. Troy held his big body gracefully, and Nancy's head was back, her eyes laughing and shining, never leaving his smiling face. Around the edges of the floor the skaters clapped and tapped out the beat, calling encouragement, cheering.

Troy tightened his hold. She was like a feather in his embrace, responding to every slightest move his body ordered. He kept his eyes on hers, on the tilted-back face. Nancy closed her eyes, borne up in the hold of something so great, so powerful, that she could not have resisted had she wanted. Troy's arms were firm, no trembling in them, and he held her tightly in place, commanding her every movement, her very breathing.

Troy's blood fired and came surging through his body, up his long legs, across his flat belly into his chest, filling his arms and warming, alive and potent in his loins. His dancing increased with the rebirth of passion and fervor, and, as the music crashed to a rocketing finale, he caught her, dragging her against him, finding her lips and holding his mouth on hers, trapping her captive, unheeding of the shouts, the cheers and the screams from the racketing audience in the circle.

The tap on his shoulder broke the moment. Troy's lifting gaze came to rest on the sneering face of Harry Marvel.

"You kids are damn good," Harry admitted, the cigar bobbing with his words. "Only how's about knockin' off the lovin'-up bit, huh? This here's a respectable place. Might give the other kids ideas."

Before Troy could lash out with a retort, Harry Marvel had drifted on, heading for the back of the place and the john.

Nancy laughed and reached up, catching his chin, turning his bright-eyed, flushed face down to her. "Never mind, honey," She smiled. "He's jealous, that's all."

"Wow! You two ought to go professional!" Billy Joe and his Cora Sue had rolled up to their side. The girls exchanged brief nods and Billy Joe's hand clapped Troy's shoulder. "That calls for a drink, I'd say."

"I ... I haven't any," Troy grunted, his eyes avoiding Nancy's look.

"All by yourself! Already?" Billy Joe was astonished. "Gees, man!"

"I ... I spilled it, knocked it over," Troy supplied lamely.

He shot an offhand look at Nancy. She was not looking at him. She and Cora Sue were busy talking.

"Well, come on. There's plenty. We'll all have a snort." Billy Joe pressured Troy's arm. "Girls? Drink?"

"I don't want any, thanks, Billy Joe," Nancy declined. The two girls had those looks on their faces, the kind of apprehension mixed with martyred resignation at the doings of men. "You two go on, have your drink. It's all right," she added hastily.

"Okay?" Billy Joe glanced at his date.

"Okay." The tall girl nodded. "Only don't be too long, huh?"

"Just a few minutes."

The girls moved off the floor together, going toward the steps into the bleachers. Troy and Billy Joe skated slowly around the perimeter of the floor, heading to the back of the place. They threaded their way through the mob and went out to the parking lot, to Billy Joe's car. Each of them took a good drink, standing by the car. The night was cooler; the stars overhead flung against the black of the moonless sky in a splash of glitter.

After a moment Troy took his troubled eyes from the lighted back door to the rink. "You see Rita Karnes around lately?" he asked quietly.

"Rita? You mean Marvel's girl?"

"Yeah."

"Saw her come in earlier, seen her talkin' with him."

"I mean, later. Recently."

Billy Joe eyed Troy speculatively. "No, I seen her talkin' with Marvel, then I ain't seen her since." There was a pause. "Why?"

"Nothin'."

"You been horsin' around that?" Billy Joe didn't wait for his answer. "No wonder Marvel's been pickin' on you!"

"He ain't been pickin' on me."

"He was up tryin' to get friendly with Nancy when you was out gettin' Cokes," Billy Joe said meaningfully.

Troy flashed a sharp glance at his friend. "What do you mean, tryin' to get friendly?"

"He was makin' with the talk when I come in. Reckon I kinda busted that up quick."

"He best keep to himself, he knows what's good for him," Troy muttered grimly.

"He didn't do nothin', say nothin'. Don't get yourself all in an uproar. Just gab, that's all." Billy Joe waved the little bottle. "You want another shot?" When Troy shook his head, Billy Joe slowly screwed the cap back. Without looking up he cleared his throat. "You wasn't by any chance spillin' that bottle of yours with somebody else?"

"What's that supposed to mean?"

Billy Joe's face was grave in the half-light from the distant doorway. "I mean, it wasn't you and that Rita dame maybe havin' drinks together," he suggested blandly.

Troy's flush betrayed him. "Maybe," he grunted.

"Man, oh man, you ain't got no sense!" Billy Joe exploded. "You start hookin' 'round with Harry Marvel's girl, you're askin' for trouble all the way." He stared at Troy in disbelief. "What's the goddam hell matter with you, Troy? You got yourself the nicest dish in town and you go fartin' 'round some damn whore who'll only bring you a mess of trouble!"

"I don't know." Troy turned away helplessly. "I got with her one night not long ago, just one of them things. I reckoned maybe we could do a repeat, I don't know what come over me. I was wrong. The liquor, maybe."

"Man, you sure got me fooled. All these years I been thinkin' you had all the brains on the South Plains. You ain't got nothin' up there but rocks!"

Troy bit the edge of his lip. "You ain't tellin' me nothin' I don't know."

Billy Joe pulled open the car door, leaned in and replaced the bottle in the compartment. He slammed the cover shut, closed the door and stepped back, bringing his full attention to his friend with worried eyes. "Look, Troy boy, I ain't passin' out no advice. You're sure as hell old enough to do what you want and I reckon as how you'll do it; only doin' it with Rita Karnes when Harry Marvel's just 'round the corner don't make good sense. I don't trust that guy; you get him riled up and anything can happen."

"I can take care of myself," Troy countered truculently.

"Horseshit!" Billy Joe snorted. "You start screwin' 'round Harry Marvel's dame, you ain't takin' very good care of nothin'."

"Well," Troy shifted uncomfortably, "reckon we ought to be gettin' on back."

"Yeah," Billy Joe agreed. "You better be stayin' with your girl, you want a tip from me."

Billy Joe led the way across the lot, Troy trailing after him. They did not speak until after they had clumped through the back door and had come to the fringe of the skating floor. Troy's eyes roamed in spite of his control. Rita must have gone on home or somewheres. She was nowhere in sight. He and Billy Joe stood side by side, looking up to where the girls sat chatting together on the bleacher tier.

"That Cora Sue's quite a dish," Troy ventured.

"She's fun," Billy Joe said simply, "that's all, just fun."

Troy got the unspoken crack. He made no reply. Taking the lead he worked his way toward the steps. Billy Joe came behind, his troubled eyes on the back of his friend. As they came to the steps, Billy Joe glanced off across the floor to the entrance. Harry Marvel had not returned. The young guy in the levis still sat with his leg posted up like that. Billy Joe sighed and followed Troy up the dangerous steps, testing each skate-wheeled stop before he set his full weight on the foot.

Just before they came to the girls, Troy stopped and waited for Billy Joe. In a low voice Troy made his request. "Look, kid, if Rita shows up, asks you anything about where I am or anything, kiss her off for me, huh? You don't know nothin'...."

"Check. Now you're showin' some sense. I'm good at that ... not knowin' nothin'." Billy Joe stepped ahead and grinned down at his date. "Come on, cookie, break up the big woman talk. You and me got some skatin' to do."

Immediately Cora Sue came to her feet, reaching out to steady herself on Billy Joe's arm. As the couple came past Troy standing there in the aisle, Billy Joe's glance flickered across his friend's face.

"Get smart, chum," he barked crisply, "be grateful for what you got."

Troy flushed. He pushed on past them and slid on to the broad bleacher seat. He groped for Nancy's hand and brought it to his lap, sandwiching it between his palms. Together they silently watched as Cora Sue and Billy Joe took the floor, joined the crowd.

"They go good together," Troy said.

"They're a nice pair," Nancy commented soberly. "They like each other, but they aren't serious. They just have a good time."

"Don't we have a good time?" Troy demanded. "Don't we?"

"Yes, sure, Troy ..." Nancy faltered. "Only, with us, well, it's different."

There was a kind of upended appeal in her words, a tentative questioning. Troy grinned and caught her against his side impulsively. "Sure," he agreed, "sure thing, with us it's different, I reckon."

The vague remembrance of those few rocketing moments with Rita came back shadowy and indistinct in his mind. He glanced over the top of Nancy's head, seeking the front of the hall. Harry Marvel was still absent from his post. Troy worked his mouth, trying to rid himself of the returned scummy feeling, the memory of Rita's fighting mouth. He moved away from Nancy and reached out, catching her hands. "Let's get out of here," he urged. "Let's get goin', honey!"

"It's still early yet," she protested dubiously.

"It's gettin' too damn hot in here, sticky."

She nodded slowly. "Whatever you want, Troy, you know that."

He brightened instantly. He put his arm around her, guiding her carefully down the steps. Along the fringe of the skating throng he kept his arm around her, leading her along toward the exit passage. The guy in the levis was still in command. Neither Troy nor Nancy knew him and, as they approached, he lolled back in the chair, tilting, and lifted his leg, swinging it out of their way so they could skate on past him.

In the equipment room Nancy seated herself and Troy kneeled to help remove her skates. In a moment he had them off, sat beside her and got rid of his own. He was gone a moment to the desk, turned in the skates and came back with their shoes. Without speaking he bent forward and worked to put them on.

"Hope nothin' I said's drivin' you off early," Harry Marvel said distinctly.

Troy finished with his shoe and straightened, his eyes narrowing. The big man stood directly in front of them, breathing heavily, standing with his thick legs spread apart, looking down at them with an odd, metallic-looking gleam in his eyes.

"You had nothin' to do with it," Troy lied in a low voice.

"Wouldn't want it to be that way," Harry Marvel said. He took his eyes from Troy and gazed openly at Nancy. "Like I been sayin', kid, you're the best-lookin' little skater here tonight. You keep thinkin' over what I was sayin' about them contests. Way I see it, you might could win hands down."

"You ain't got nothin' she wants," Troy stormed.

Harry turned his little gimlet eyes with the funny look on the taller man. "Could be you could be surprised," he countered coolly.

"You ain't got no surprises, Marvel!" Troy answered.

"Might could be you'll get surprised one of these here days," Harry hinted. He had not taken those funny eyes off Troy. There was no warmth in his look; it was a kind of dead look, yet there was that scalelike metallic cast in it.

"I'll be waitin'," Troy said.

"I'm all ready," Nancy stood hastily. She clutched at Troy's arm, her apprehensive glance on the full, reddish face in front of them. Troy made no move. She felt the hard-ening of his muscles in his forearm and knew he stood with his fists balled, watching the other man angrily. "Come on, Troy," she urged, pulling at him.

Responding to her insistence, Troy moved. He brushed past Harry Marvel, letting his big body be propelled toward the street entrance. At the doorway he turned and glanced back. Harry Marvel stood as they had left him, only his body had swung at the waist as he had watched them go. The ugly lips had thinned down and the cigar end had returned to its accustomed place. The eyes still held that unnatural look in them.

Nancy worked with speed. She wanted Troy out of there, out and away before any blow-off came. Once Troy's temper got the best of him, anything could happen. Even now she could see the nervous tic in his cheek, see the faint, bluish smudges of the old bruises near the eyes, the reminder of the fight with his brother.

On the sidewalk in front of the skating rink, Troy took a deep steeling breath. The cool night air went racing down into the cavity of his chest and brought some calm. He itched to go back and take a poke at that big bastard inside. Nancy had linked her arm firmly through his and she drew him steadily, leading him to the parking lot back of the building.

At the side of the car she stopped, reached around him and caught the still-tensed body in her arms, drawing him close. "It wouldn't have done any good, Troy," she assured him breathlessly. "It wouldn't have done anything but kick up a fuss, that's all."

"He didn't have no goddam business …"

"It doesn't mean anything, honest, Troy."

Troy swallowed. He straightened a little. "I'm all right, Nance, honest. Let's get goin'."

# CHAPTER TWELVE

Troy let the car have its own lead. He drove slowly, his left hand monitoring the wheel, his right arm around Nancy's shoulders, keeping her body close, fitted against him. Every now and then a stray wisp of her fine hair reached out like a tendril, finding his flesh, snagging on the faint, rough bristle of his beard. The fires of his anger had burned low and only the dull, distant throbbing in his head remained. She'd been right, he thought, nothing could have come from hanging around any longer.

"Want somethin' to eat or anything?"

Nancy murmured something unintelligible. He grinned at her as they waited for the light to change. "Hey, you," he reached and raised her chin a little. "I said, you hungry or anything?"

"No," she murmured drowsily, snuggling back against him. "Let's just drive like this. This is what I like to do."

Troy shrugged. This is what he liked to do, too. He released the brake as the green came flashing on and the car rolled casually down the length of the broad arterial. As they neared the intersection of the highway through town, Troy glanced down again. She had her eyes closed and her hand had come up and her fingers now toyed aimlessly with a button on his shirt.

There was a tightening in his stomach muscles and a binding, gathering slow and steady in his loins. Without saying anything he guided the car along the white curving line between the traffic islands and headed the machine down the long straight stretch of the tree-lined highway with its big houses set far back, pointing the car toward the distant bright lights of the hospital and the open black of the fields and the skies beyond.

As the car bumped and jogged across the intersecting railroad tracks at the junction, Nancy gave herself a little shove and sat up straight. She brushed her hair back and peered out, then glanced through the half-light at Troy.

"Where we goin'?"

"Just ridin', like you wanted," Troy answered. "Any ideas?"

Nancy said nothing. She fought off the assailing touch of inexplicable apprehension. Somehow the lights of the city thrown up against the sky behind them seemed remote, slipping away, out of reach.

"Well," he probed quietly.

"No," She shook her head, her eyes rounding on the straight marking line leveling off in front of them. "I don't care," she said low.

She did care. She did not come back to his side, but sat off now in the corner of the broad seat, the hard, reassuring thrust of the car door handle cutting into the soft flesh at her side. In the occasional burst of illumination from the lights of a passing car, she could see Troy's head in sharp relief. He was driving casually, guiding the car at cruising speed, his eyes quiet now, thoughtful on the stretch of the road. In a little while they had left the houses behind; there was nothing to be seen on either side of the broad highway but the black, bleak, dead cotton fields. Far off in the distance was the dull glow where the air base kept its vigil. Low against the horizon was the blinking light of a slow-moving star, the late plane from Abilene and Dallas, heading across to the north of the city and the airport.

"Come back, little Sheba," Troy chuckled. His big arm reached for her, his fingers feeling.

She knew she ought to remind him that it was getting late, that maybe they ought to turn back, head back to the city, to the lights and the security and protection that lay under the glowing cowl of the sky. His fingers caught the fleshy portion of her arm and weakly she allowed herself to let her body slide across the seat, taking her place in the hollow of him, receiving the beating warmth of him against her.

They rode silently. Troy held her close, his fingertips barely touching the fabric of her blouse, close to her swelling breast. She lay against him, her eyes closed, feeling the feathery touch, feeling the awakening insistence of her body to his touch, not caring now, letting the little fires come to touch the nerve ends of her being.

Some moments past the intersection to the air base, Troy pulled the car off the road and guided the machine along the rutted, twin paths of car tracks that led into the dark and desolate turn row close to the abandoned old gin. For an instant the lights of the car caught the whole of the field in a sweeping arc, bringing the dead stalks of last year's harvest sharp and spiny white, like scattered matchsticks in the glare. He reached down and snapped off the lights, cut the engine and let the darkness and the stillness come flooding the car. They were caught up in a thick, muffling velvet fold of silence against which their quickened breathing rose.

She had not opened her eyes. She had felt the sudden swerving of the car that brought her hard against him and now in the silence and the stillness she held herself alert, not taking herself from him, waiting dry-lipped and tense.

Troy shifted in the seat, moving her a little forward, trying to work his leg down the seat length, bringing her between. Somehow they arranged themselves as easily as if this were an often experienced thing, a familiar, intimate recurrence.

She felt her head lifting, her chin caught in the cup of his palm, and then his lips came down on hers, cutting off reason, cutting off her breath, bringing a wildness in a whirlwind spinning through her.

Troy came forward, bending her head back against the seat, his lips hard and demanding against hers, his breath hot against her cheek, his tongue a sudden, wonderous, alive thing, forcing, demanding.

"Troy!" she moaned, her body caught up in the capturing demands. "Oh, Troy! Troy! Troy!"

The mushroom blast rose swiftly, a blinding, brilliant, all-encompassing thing in her of heat and flesh and wanting. Reason was stripped away by the seeking, clutching hands upon her. There was the hard moving thrust of him, the touch of him on her aching breasts. She cried out once, thrusting him from her, and the great, hollowed feeling in the midst of her, the thing of hunger and need for which she knew no name, gave strength to her hands. They went forth without command, catching at his shirt, stripping away the fastenings, baring his chest to her fingers, to her palms. She knew the pimpled buttons of his nipples, felt the silk and wire of his chest hairs. She felt for him by raw instinct, by the insatiable knowledge of sense alone.

It was Troy who suddenly took himself from her. He moved back sharply, taking his body from her touch. The withdrawal was abrupt, bringing her to instant pause as they fell back away from each other, their eyes closed, their breathing harsh and rasping, deep draughts of expending passion.

Troy glanced at her. She sat now straight, stiff, her hands in her lap, staring blindly out across the fields, her gaze far out to where the tiny red lights of the air base hangar roof blinked erratically in the blackness. He swallowed and reached forth, touching for a moment the moist coolness of her arm. She said nothing, made no move. In a moment she took her arm from his touch and there was a kind of strangled whimper in her throat.

"Nance ... I—I'm sorry ..." He fumbled.

She shook her head and wet her lips. "Not your fault," she managed hoarsely.

Her eyes in the shadows were concealed from him, eyes that mirrored the open acknowledgment, the recognition of herself, of their twinship in desire, Troy and herself. She saw now with the eyes of the woman she had become and she knew the harsh insistence of her love for this man.

Troy brought his troubled gaze to the big hands helpless in his lap. In him there was a soreness, a core of hurt and bruising, the gnaw of frustration. The slightest whisper of the wind through the chinks of the closed window at his side brought awareness back to him. He looked again across the chasm that lay between them. "Nance?"

Her head turned sightly. In the gloom he could see her eyes on him, dull and glazed.

"It's time we got goin', I reckon," he said. "I ..."

"No." She knew what he was going to say, put forth her hand to stop him. "Don't say anything, Troy," she faltered. "There isn't much to say." She suddenly picked up strength in her voice. "You see, I wanted it to happen with you. I wanted it to happen."

Her voice broke suddenly, shattering with a fragile tinkling, and she came forward, catching her head in her open palms, covering her face with the young fingers. There was the sound of her weeping, muffled and strained.

"Nance! Nance, I love you!" Troy's voice burst forth in a cry and his hands caught at her shoulders. He turned her to him, forced her masking fingers away. "Nance, we'll get married. I been plannin' we'd get married someday, you know that!" His voice gained speed and strength, as if in the moment he had at last stumbled over the sought-for key, was frantically now work-ing to unlock the last remaining door to the future.

She had raised her face slowly, brought her tear-stained face into the dusky light of the car. Her eyes searched his face ear-nestly, intently, desperately seeking the truth.

"Marry?" she repeated wonderingly. "You want to marry me, Troy?"

His spirit soared swiftly under the explosive release. "Of course, honey ... we'll get married, soon. Hell, we can be mar-ried, even if I'm goin' off to college! Other couples get married that way!"

Married. It had come to pass, after all. They'd be married and alone, the way she had dreamed about, married with a place of their own somewhere, no more hasty good nights, no more fears and no more wanting. It would be she and Troy all the time, together always, the hold of his big arms around her, and she would be free from being afraid and shame and the unfulfilled longings.

"Smile now?"

Troy had come close to her again. She retreated a little. He laughed then, the old, assured laugh, and tipped her chin up. He came bending down and kissed her lightly, without seeking.

"You'll see, Nance, everything will be all right, everything'll be fine." He grinned suddenly, his straight, strong teeth bright white even here in the darkness of the car. "There won't be any more foolin' around on back roads no more for us!"

He slid back now to his familiar place under the wheel and almost feverishly he started the car. He raced the engine for a moment, then threw the car into a lurching, jerking half-circle through the ruts of the unplowed field until the wheels found the tracks that led back to the paved highway. There was a pause at the edge of the paving, while Troy let a speeding car heading west flash by. Then he threw the car into gear, the tires squeal-ing as they spurted from dirt to asphalt. Troy reached down and snapped on the radio switch. The selector band glowed brightly and, in a moment, the all-night disk jockey program came on. The car interior was throbbing with the breathless beat of the quick-tempoed music.

Troy fished in his slacks for the cigarette pack. He took one dexterously with one hand and stuck it between his lips. He groped for the dash lighter and, when it was ready, pressed the red-eyed whorl against the cigarette until it was lit. As he replaced the lighter, his eyes rose to the rear-view mirror and he noticed the lights of the car following behind them, realized that the car was simply trailing them, making no attempt to catch up and pass.

Troy took the cigarette from his lips. He kept his eyes on those lights. Funny, he thought, there had been no car coming, no sign of lights when he had turned on to the highway from the road to the old gin. There had only been that other car, the one going west, in the opposite direction from town.

Silently he watched the headlamps. Maybe the car had been parked along the side of the highway somewhere, had started up behind them as they passed. Probably nothing but a couple of kids out having some loving by themselves. Still, as he drove, tak-ing infrequent puffs from the cigarette, not talking to her, not hearing any more the blare of music from the radio, he kept his eyes pinned on the lights of the car behind. Something disturbed him. There had been no car coming in from the west when he had come on to the highway and he knew damned well he had not passed a car parked on the shoulder from the moment he had started on the way home.

The lights from the dashboard caught in the reddish short hairs on Harry Marvel's fingers, sparking and glinting in them curled and gripped on the rung of the steering wheel. He sat forward on the car seat, hunched up close to the wheel, his eyes never leaving the twin beacons of the tail lights of the car ahead. His thick, full, sensual lips were compressed and, as he drove in the silent, gliding machine, the only sound was the faint singing of the tires on the pavement and the heavy measured rasp of his breath.

He wore no jacket, and he had taken off his shirt, despite the cold. Dirt streaked the T-shirt and hardened under his nails, though he was not conscious of these. Though the little cotton shirt offered scant protection from the chill of the night breezes, Harry was not conscious of the cold. His entire attention was centered on the car ahead; his only movements during the brief ride down the highway to town was the easy guiding of the powered wheel.

As the two cars entered the city limits Harry slackened his speed. He coasted along, keeping the car ahead in sight, letting it get a block, two blocks ahead on the deserted street.

It was when the two cars approached the main intersection at the edge of the college campus that their courses divided. Troy Bannock's car swung to the right, heading down the arterial avenue toward the darkened residential section. Harry Marvel guided his machine to the left, skirting the traffic islands, turning the nose of the car toward the skating rink on the north side of town. He twisted his head as he made the turn, caught the last glimpse of the flickering tail lights of the other car as it moved swiftly down the stretch of the street.

It was only then that the expression on Harry Marvel's face broke. His lips parted slightly and his tongue-tip moved along the edges, moistening them. He twisted his left arm slightly, catching the gold of the watch numerals in the dash light reflection, squinting his little eyes to make out the time. There wasn't so long to go now, an hour or so before the rink closed. He'd put in the rest of the shift himself.

He felt tired, bushed, as if he had been working at lifting all night. He thought vaguely of his bed in the small apartment and the feel of it and her next to him and wondered if he could take the rest of the time off from the rink. The lips compressed themselves again and Harry's grip again tightened on the wheel. As he watched the lights of the big building come up on the left side of the street, he knew he could take the rest of the time all right. This wasn't the time for crapping out; what he had to do meant keeping on your toes. He'd put in his time, the hour or so, and then he'd close up the joint at the regular hour and then he'd go home and then he'd go to bed. After that there'd be time for lots of sacking out, lots of time.

All through the ride into town Nancy had sat back against the seat watching the play of lights on Troy's face. There was a rich contentment in her. She wondered what he was thinking about as he sat there, guiding the car easily, taking an infrequent drag on the cigarette, staring ahead, glancing occasionally into the rear-view mirror, the lights from the car behind them casting an illuminating flash, like a band, across his eyes. She wondered if he were thinking of how it was going to be, just the two of them, belonging together, being together.

He sat back on the way home, guiding the car easily, letting the machine make its way at a casual speed. The window was down and the freshened breeze washed across his face, wiping away the dull drugged feeling of over-whelming fatigue. Only his mind was active, reaching back through the kaleidoscopic events of the night, remembering, sorting.

At the turn off to the place he sat up. There were no lights. The old house sat high, etched in black against the dark purple, star-flecked backdrop.

Troy cut the engine as he came to the building and coasted silently, easing the car around until it came to the open area in front of the barn. He switched off the lights and sat for a moment, his hands on the rim of the wheel. The whole place was still in the death of sleep. Only the rising northern wind spanked against the weathered walls of the barn, came funneling down over the car.

Troy got out and eased the car door shut. He came around the end of the machine and started across the open break of the yard. Somewhere, off in the distance, a stray paper caught up in the eddies of the breeze went scraping along the hard ground, scuffing and rasping as it skittered.

At the first of the steps, Troy stopped. He turned, his hand on the rough grain of the railing, and faced the wind. There was a good clean feel to it. He reached up slowly and undid the buttons of his shirt, pulling the fabric aside, letting the breeze find his flesh to wash and cool. After a moment he took his hand away and started up the stairs. Midway he eased himself down carefully, and hunching forward he took out a cigarette and lit it. He sat smoking, letting his gaze wander.

"I don't suppose you got another one of them?"

He started sharply. Cressy was on the landing, her hair pinned in place, her full body caught up in the familiar terrycloth robe. He stared at her. "What the hell you doin' prowlin' 'round this time of night?"

"Just gimme the cigarette, Troy," she said wearily, coming down the first two steps to seat herself, tucking the robe in close around her legs.

Silently Troy handed the single cigarette from the pack.

"You afraid maybe the pack'll get away?"

Troy eyed her sullenly. She had her elbow on her knee, sat holding the cigarette extended, waiting. "I reckon you want a light, too," he asked unpleasantly.

"If it ain't too much out of your way, sir," she snapped.

His eyes met hers through the flaring yellow glare of the flame. She looked tired. "How come you're wanderin' 'round the middle of the night?" he asked again. "You and Tom have a fight or somethin'?"

"Tom and I don't have fights," she countered shortly. She picked a fleck of tobacco from her lip and flicked it off into the darkness. "We let you take care of that department," she added.

Troy's eyes narrowed on her face. Suddenly he spoke. "You really go for that guy, don't you?" he asked quietly.

"Tom?" She turned surprised eyes on him. "I married him," she qualified simply.

"Lots of people get married," Troy commented. The unspoken thought was there.

"I think you'll find most of them love each other, Troy," she offered. "Those who don't have a pretty rough road ahead."

Troy lapsed into silence. He saw that she was barefoot, her nails pale and uncolored, like little coins spread out on the stained wood of the old step. "How was the movie?"

"The movie?" She took a drag from the cigarette and shrugged. "Oh, so-so. June Allyson and her little girl face and that Italian character, the handsome one I can't understand half the time. Ma seemed to like it," she added.

" 'Interlude,' " Troy said.

"What?"

" 'Interlude,' that was the name of the picture."

"Oh." Cressy eyed him through a fresh plume of smoke. Troy always knew everything, quick as a flash, no matter what was said about anything Troy always knew the answers. Sometimes it got annoying. "I never remember the names," she supplied defiantly.

"I know," he responded silkily.

Cressy pulled the robe a little closer around her shoulders, covering over her chest where the cool breeze sought entry. "You have a good time in town?"

Troy bridled. "What you want, a complete report or somethin'?"

Cressy turned and cocked her head. She thought she heard someone inside. "I was only askin'," she protested low. "And keep your voice down, you want the whole house out here?"

"Might as well, then I could tell 'em all at once!" he grumped.

Cressy sighed. She slumped a little. "I was only askin'," she repeated dully.

Troy felt suddenly abashed. He hadn't meant to bite her head off. He cleared his throat. "I had a good time, Cressy," he offered with surprising gentleness.

"See Nancy?"

"Yeah."

She said nothing and he glanced at her. It was unusual, her not asking what they had done.

"We went skatin'," he offered.

She eyed him thoughtfully, took a final drag on the cigarette and flicked the butt far out in the yard. A spray of sparks fanned across the darkness and died, leaving only the single dull red coal to die unattended. "It's funny," she remarked quietly, "the way you kids go skatin' so much 'round here. Down in Dallas I don't think I ever had anyone ask me to go skatin' ever."

"We get our kicks." Troy shrugged.

"I guess so." She watched as he ground the stub of the cigarette into the step plank. "How's Nancy?"

"She's fine."

"She's a nice girl," Cressy said quietly. "She's a real nice girl, Troy."

He poked at the mashed end of the cigarette with the toe of his shoe. "Cressy," he said suddenly, "there's somethin' I been meanin' to say to you."

She turned her head, her gaze cautious on his profile. "Yeah?"

He turned halfway on the step and his hand touched hers on her knee. "I know I been a bastard to you sometimes, only I ain't meant it like I sounded and acted." He swallowed and avoided her eyes. "I think Tom's mighty damn lucky havin' you, that's what I'm meanin'." He bit the inside of his upper lip and turned away from her sparkling eyes in confusion.

Cressy sat immobile. He had taken his hand from the brief touch and he sat turned back, staring out over the formless fields. After a moment or two she found her voice. "Somethin's happened to you, Troy, somethin's finally got inside you at last," she said wonderingly.

"I just didn't mean to go hurtin' you, is all," he countered gruffly. "I just been speakin' out and actin' without thinkin', is all."

She set her feet down on the stair below and clasped her hands loosely in her lap, sat looking down on them. "What happened tonight, Troy?" she asked softly.

For once there was no bridling anger in him at the intrusion. He sat quietly, looking into the darkness beyond, and knew that he had wanted her to ask this time. It was a totally new, strange thing to him, this wanting to be asked. Slowly he turned and looked at her profile, at the small ear and the firm, yet delicate line of her jaw. "I reckon as how Nance and me's plannin' to get married," he announced quietly.

She looked up then quickly, with the bright light springing into her eyes, and her hands came from her lap and caught his and held them. "Oh, Troy," she breathed. "Oh, Troy, I'm so glad! Oh, you're right, Troy, you ain't makin' any mistakes this time!"

He flushed and looked down at her hold on him. "I don't know why," he said slowly, "suddenly, sittin' here like this, I wanted you to know first; somehow I suddenly felt you'd understand, maybe even more'n the others, in a way."

"Thanks, Troy," she breathed softly. She gave his hands a squeeze and then let go. "I won't say anything to the others, not until you have a chance."

"Thanks."

She looked down at the foot of the steps thoughtfully. "What about your goin' off to college?"

"We could do it, if I go. Others do. If we get married, Nance could go with me. Maybe it'd be fun, fun for both of us."

Cressy sat still for a long moment. There was nothing more to say. Her whole insides went out to the big boy beside her. The barriers were down between them at last and she kept her shining eyes on him. "I reckon it's time to be hittin' the hay," she said lightly. She paused and got to her feet and looked down on him. "I'll be sayin' good night, Troy … and thanks again, thanks for everything."

"Forget it."

He sat quietly until he heard her padding footsteps go to the landing, heard the soft whine of the back door, knew she was inside. His eyes rose and once again he looked at the shining glitter of the spangled skies. Somehow, sitting here like this, he saw the stars brighter than they had ever been before and inside him there was a gleaming, clean feeling that, too, had never before been there.

# CHAPTER THIRTEEN

The first April Sunday came late to the Bannock place. It came late, dawdling casually across the ocean of fields to inspect the farm buildings with lazy, impersonal curiosity, feeding its growing light to the countryside with a little less haste than weekdays, spending the Sabbath minutes without pressure.

Lying there, with his eyes shelled against the glare of the morning, Troy suddenly remembered his father and the ride back from town ... my God, was it only yesterday? He frowned, trying to recapture his father's words. His father had talked about him and Ma, Troy remembered now. He'd talked about how wild he'd been, and how he'd chased after everything he could get only, when he had met Ma, all of a sudden it had become different somehow. What was it Pa had said about getting married and all?

"When the right one comes along, it's different, you'll see," Pa had said.

Troy smiled faintly, his eyes closed, his head still turned on the pillow. Yesterday he'd thought Pa was losing his marbles, yakking about him and Ma like that; a few hours later and he knew what Pa had been talking about, all of it! It was funny how things came about. He moved slightly in the warm trough of the bed. He could see Nancy's face lighted with the glow of her love, feel the comforting reassurance of that love in her body beside him, know the full giving that was in her, waiting for him to take. There was a sting behind his closed lids and he rolled his head back and forth on the pillow.

"Oh, Pa," he whispered. "You was right, Pa, and I didn't know!"

"Troy? Hey, Troy, you awake?"

His brother's voice was husky in the mornings, thick with the sleep that took an hour or so to dissipate.

"Yeah, I'm awake," Troy grunted.

"It's gettin' late. You best get a shag on!"

"Okay." Troy shrugged. Tom had made no attempt to open the door. In a moment the older brother's boots went clumping down the hall toward the kitchen and Troy could hear the distant murmur of voices.

He shoved himself on his elbows and met his own gaze in the mirror beyond the foot of the bed. He looked tired this morning; the faint bluish smudges had all but disappeared in the passing days. He touched the cut on his eyebrow gingerly; it was almost healed up. His mind skittered off to the thought of Sunday and church. He groaned audibly. He didn't like church much; he never felt like going to hear Joe Ben Potter's sermons. Only Pa might not be active in the church, but he took a dim view of any of them skipping church, unless they had a damn good reason. You just went, that was all!

"Troy? You comin' soon?"

Momentary irritation swept his face as Cressy's voice shrilled through the closed door.

"Yeah, for God's sake, I'm comin'," he snapped.

"It's Sunday," she warned.

"I know it's Sunday."

"Best get goin', boy."

He stood there naked before the mirror, listening as she made her way down the hall. His thoughts went back to the conversation last night on the back porch steps and he smiled slowly. She was all right, that Cressy, for all her nosing around. He felt like a damn fool, the way he'd spoken to her, had been treating her from time to time. Somehow, last night he felt he'd gotten to know her for the first time, really. Somehow, he could see how goddam lucky Tom was.

Through habit he moved closer to the window, bent down and peered out across the fields, lifting his eyes to the skies. There were a few scattered clouds wandering aimlessly in from the west and already the sunlight through the window was warm on the flesh of his chest and belly. It warmed up quick, once April got underway; pretty soon there'd be rain, if they were lucky, rain and lightning and thunder and maybe the tornadoes would come before long, too.

Troy said nothing about the decision that he and Nancy Collins had made the night before. Only once did Cressy meet his gaze across the table and then there was only the faintest shadow of a smile reflected in her eyes. He averted his gaze and went on eating, grateful for her silence.

Will Bannock never ate heavily. He picked at his food, ate enough to keep him going, then sat back and watched the others as they worked through the big meals. His eyes wandered this Sunday morning over the faces of his family. There was Bess, getting older, kindness and devotion to her family shining full in her face. There was Tom, sober, sincere, hard-working, and his wife, Cressy, quiet, respectful and helpmate already. And there was Troy, the youngest.

His eyes narrowed a little as he studied Troy. The boy looked tired, only somehow it was a different kind of tiredness for the usual Sunday morning. It was a relaxed kind of tiredness, and the boy's eyes were clear. He remembered listening as the boy came in last night. He had come quietly, almost noiselessly and there had been no scuffing of clothing against the doors, no bumping into little objects along the way. Will frowned faintly; something must have happened last night, he judged, something a little different, something that still sat on the boy's mind from the look on his face.

"Weather's warmin' up, Pa," Tom ventured finally.

Will took his gaze from Troy's bowed head and his brows lifted. "I was thinkin' it had got warmer. Can't always be sure."

"Sure has, Pa, temperature's gone right up."

"Gets warmer and stays warmer, we're like to get us some rain," Will observed hopefully.

"Get a pack of dust along with it," Troy grunted.

"Wonder if there'll be many twisters this year?" Tom asked.

"Never can tell 'bout them things 'round these here parts," Will mused. "Some years is bad; others nothin' much happens. Last year wasn't so bad."

"This year'll probably be a heller!" Troy prophesied grimly.

"Troy!"

"Sorry, Ma."

Ma Bannock crossed to the stove and began to straighten things up. She paused and glanced out of the kitchen window over the broad yard to the mounded hump of the tornado shelter, to the weather-beaten double doors that closed over the top. "Most time I was gettin' out there cleanin' up that dugout," she observed calmly. "First thing you know, we might have to use it!"

"Sure hope I never have to go through one of 'em," Cressy breathed fervently.

Will Bannock smiled indulgently at his daughter-in-law. "Might could be you will, sooner or later, so long as you're livin' here. Them that lives in tornado alley has a right to be expectin' such things."

"Tornado alley ..." She eyed her father-in-law speculatively. "Pa, how come they call it that? I've heard that before."

Will shrugged. "Just a name some feller gave it, I reckon. Seems like there's a part of the country from Kansas somewhere runnin' down through West Texas and cuttin' over through to East Texas that some feller once called tornado alley 'cause there was so many of the goldanged things 'round these parts. I reckon as how the name just stuck." He belched lightly, bringing his hand up tardily, with a guilty glance at Ma. "Don't mean much, 'pears to me, damn things keep happenin' all over the country these days, if a feller's gonna believe what he reads."

Ma had turned from the stove and she had frowned at his curse word. Will's face was bland; she knew he had not meant it as such. Everything this mornin' was too nice to spoil; she let it pass.

The preacher, Joe Ben Potter, and his bride-to-be, the widow Martha Dovely, came to Sunday dinner. It was during the meal that the interruption came. The seven had finished all but the pie and coffee when the car came thundering around the house and spluttered to a stop close by the back porch. Little spurts of dust puffing through the half-opened kitchen window. The table conversation died away and they sat, not eating, simply listening. There was the slam of the car door, the sound of scuffing steps on the earth and steps mounting the back steps.

"Land sakes," Ma blurted. "Now who on earth can be comin' 'round this time of day?"

From his place Troy commanded the best view of the back doorway. He saw Billy Joe Everett come to the first of the double doors, hesitate and then knock, not too heavily. Puzzled he shoved back his chair and stood, catching their attention. "It's Billy Joe, Ma, reckon he wants to see me." He hesitated and looked at the others. " 'Scuse me," he murmured.

There was a muttered conversation between the two young men on the back porch, too low and indistinct for the others to hear. Then the two moved down the steps and walked slowly across the hard pan to the car.

"Seems like Troy could have had his friend come 'round at a decent hour, when folks is done with their Sunday eatin'," Ma grumbled testily.

"Maybe they got a date or somethin'," Tom suggested blandly.

"Troy could have said somethin', if that's so," Will commented slowly, his eyes still on the doorway.

"It ain't nothin', I'm sure," Cressy offered quietly.

"So?" Troy had stopped in front of the car and he frowned at Billy Joe.

The other scratched his lean, hairless chest, and his eyes were troubled. "So ... I just reckoned you ought to know, for Christ's sake!"

Troy hunched down beside the car and picked up a bit of stick; he began to draw little circles in the sloughy earth. "You come barrel-assin' all the way out from town to tell me that that crazy Harry Marvel's been drunk, yappin' all over town about Rita and me horsin' around together."

"He ain't sayin' it just like that," Billy Joe hedged uneasily. "I seen him at the drive-in early this mornin' and he was shootin' off his mouth so you could hear him down to Tahoka. That Miz Devine she had to run him off finally, swore she'd call the cops on him. He sure was real mean."

Troy came to his feet, the stick still in his hand. He snapped it between his fingers, underscoring his words. "Look, kid, stop frettin', you know Harry Marvel. He's a no-good bastard, we all know that, and he's a troublemaker, always has been. Hell, last night he gets snotty with me and Nance, I almost slugged him. That's probably what's eatin' him.... he gets a few slugs in him and anybody's a louse. All drunks do that; that's why they get tanked up, I reckon. They get a chance to say somethin' they ain't got the guts to say when they ain't drunked up."

"Well"—Billy Joe colored slightly and a sheepish look came over his face—"I was just listenin' and watchin' him and what he was sayin' about how you and Rita was havin' fun, and it didn't sound so good, not the way he was sayin' it. You know ... 'specially the way it is with you and Nancy and all."

"Forget it." Troy flicked the stick bits off into the yard. "I'm headin' in to see Nance this evenin'. Nothin's gonna change nothin'."

"Well, I reckon as how you're probably right. Reckon I just got to frettin' too much."

Troy smiled and his hand found his friend's shoulder. "That's okay, kid. I appreciate it, honest. If I hear anything, leastways I'll know where it come from."

"Sure hope it don't make no difference ... with Nancy and her folks, I mean, if they get to hearin' anything."

"People like them don't hear things punks like Harry Marvel puts out."

"Well, okay, man." Billy Joe shifted awkwardly. "That's all I come to say."

"You're a good Joe," Troy grinned. As the other turned away, he remembered. "How's about some of Ma's pie; we're just gettin' to it."

"Naw, thanks. I already had my supper."

"Okay then."

Troy remained where he was until Billy Joe was headed out toward the highway back to town. Then he started slowly toward the back steps.

That goddam Harry Marvel was a royal pain in the ass! Right now he gets himself plastered, starts shootin' off his mouth all over town, stirrin' up a stink over nothin'. Troy's fists locked and he tightened his lips. Just for one lousy stinkin' lay and now all this crap! For the moment the tidal wave of disgust for Rita, for himself, for Harry Marvel came rising swiftly. He fought against it; he'd go in and they'd talk to Nance's folks, get things set, squared away. There'd be no more Ritas, no more Harry Marvels and their big mouths, nothin' but him and Nance and all the time to come.

As he came into the kitchen, the six looked up. They had had their pie; they sat back around the table, comfortable, at ease, just gossiping Sunday-wise. Their eyes met his.

"It was nothin'," Troy brushed it off. "Just wanted me to ride over to Clovis with him."

"Not goin'?" Tom asked.

"No." Troy's eyes found Cressy. "Reckoned I'd go in and see Nance, maybe." He saw the little light shaft in her eyes and the little bob of her head.

Ma sighed. "Should have had the good manners to ask Billy Joe did he want some pie with us."

"I did, Ma … he said he already had supper."

"Nice boy, Billy Joe," Will Bannock commented. "Too bad he had to give up his schoolin'."

Mamie Collins sat in her accustomed place across the room from the TV set. Herbert Collins was deep in the soft clutch of the sofa. On a straight-backed chair between her parents, Nancy Collins watched Troy with wide, warm eyes.

Troy had delivered his brief speech standing in front of the fireplace, looking down on all three. His eyes moved from face to face, resting a little longer now and then on Nancy. Now he made a hesitant, vague motion outward from his hips with his hands.

"… and I reckon that's about it, Mr. and Mrs. Collins."

Mamie and Herbert Collins exchanged brief looks. Herbert offered no comment and Mamie knew he was waiting for her reaction.

"Well, Troy, I suppose you know this comes as no surprise," she ventured slowly. "Of course, Nancy's a little young; she's still in high school." She hesitated and the far-away memory of her own early marriage came back to her, shadowing her eyes momentarily. Then she looked across the room at Herbert, sitting so quietly, watching her with an interest she knew was both respectful and determined. She turned awkwardly in her chair and glanced at Nancy. The girl was still looking at Troy and there was no concern in her, nothing but the love she felt for this boy. There's really no question, Mamie Collins thought, they'll do as they please anyway, sooner or later. "Yes," she nodded quietly.

Herbert Collins said nothing. His eyes crinkled faintly around the corners and he glanced at his daughter. She had come to her feet quickly, had gone to her mother and leaned down and put her arms around her and kissed her. Without saying a word she came across the little space to him and he reached up and took her face between his hands and kissed her gently. "You just be happy, baby," he said huskily.

Nancy crossed and took her place at Troy's side. His big arm had come down and he lightly placed it around her waist. Mamie Collins looked at them and her eyes filled suddenly. They looked so young, so beautiful. Was there ever a time when she and Herbert had really looked like that, so fresh, so unafraid?

The older couple watched silently as Troy and Nancy went from the room. When they had gone out to the front porch and closed the front door, Mamie and Herbert Collins shared glances.

"He's such a nice-looking, clean-cut boy, Herb," she remarked quietly. "We're a couple of lucky parents, I'd say."

"I was hoping you'd feel that way," her husband said. He watched as his wife crossed the room and snapped on the TV set. She made sure the set was tuned properly, came back to her seat and settled herself with a comfortable sigh. She glanced at him and smiled. "Ed Sullivan," she said confidently.

The failing light of that Sunday brought the darkening shadows into play in the still apartment of Harry Marvel. Even in the gloom the place looked as if a tornado had passed through. There were clothes scattered everywhere. On the two chairs clothes were mounded in untidy disorder, hung on the backs, even strung from the rungs where they had caught. The floor was a messy litter, a trail of clothes that overflowed the one room and pushed on into the bathroom where the steady drip-drip of the sink faucet not quite turned off was like a marking tocsin.

There were all kinds of clothes. Here a pair of slacks, there the balled-up mound of pink panties, from the back of the chair dangled the forlorn cups of a brassiere. There was a man's suit, the trousers wadded near the bed, the coat spread arm-wide in the bathroom doorway. There were soiled jocky shorts, her blouses, his shirts, socks, stockings, shoes of both of them. The scattering storm had spared nothing.

The half-light showed him, sprawled face down on the bed, one arm crooked over the side, the fingers half-opened, the other flung out. His body lay slanting on the bed, his head partially obscured under the bunched pillow that he had shoved against the head of the bed. His face was turned so that his left cheek was on the sheet and, as he slept, his breathing came heavy and labored, rasping in the silent place. His mouth was partially open, the spittle glistening like snail tracks on the twisted, soiled sheet.

Harry Marvel slept the sleep of the drugged alcoholic, fully clad in shirt and slacks, with his shoes still on. He was stretched out exactly as he had fallen hours earlier. Close by the dangling hand was the bottle, half full, uncapped, waiting.

The man slept on. From somewhere down the street there was the single sharp blast of an automobile horn. It seemed to reach inside the shell of the man, to prick at his dead consciousness, for his mouth closed and he swallowed with difficulty, licking his thick lips, groaning slightly.

Once again the far-away horn sounded and once again he stirred. He lurched suddenly, rolling his big body over until he lay on his back. After a moment his little eyes opened and he stared dully at the muddy cream of the cheap room's ceiling.

As he lay there in the dusk, an artificial yellow from the reflection of the burning, naked globe in the bathroom, Harry had no thoughts. There was a sickness in his head, a wallowing nausea somewhere in the middle of him; the sour mash taste was in his mouth and a terrible, cottony dryness.

He brought his arms up close to his sides and pushed down, raising his body ponderously from the supine position, but the effort was too much. The blood came swiftly, brought an unbearable throb in his temples. He sank back down, working his mouth desperately against the parched agony.

He lay waiting. He blinked and with an effort turned his head to glance at his side. She was not there. He wondered where in hell she could be, gettin' up so early like this; hell, it must be just about daylight, for Christ's sake! Irritably he rolled his head, narrowing his eyes on the ceiling. She was probably filling in for some other broad down at the all-night, like she done sometimes, going right ahead doin' what she wanted, no matter what he wanted.

Harry turned his head slightly, forcing down the groan. His eyes found the lighted doorway to the bathroom. Maybe she was in there, maybe she was just sittin' there, maybe readin' like she sometimes did.

"Hey, Rita?"

The name came croaking out. It seemed to go ricocheting around the walls to come back to smite like a blow on an anvil in Harry's head. Again he tried to raise himself. Grunting, he hoisted his weight up from the flat of the mattress, peering at the doorway. As he looked down toward the floor he saw the scattered clothing in the doorway, all over the room. He scowled. Damn! she could have picked up before she went high-tailing off to work!

Propped up like that, biceps straining, he summoned his strength for the final assault. The groan burst from his lips as he forced himself to the sitting position and swung his legs from the bed. He shifted forward, catching his fiery head in his big palms, squeezing, shutting his eyes tight against the harsh pound of the blood in his brain. For some time he sat, breathing deeply, shakily, trying to force the illness down.

When he opened his eyes, his gaze fell on the half-filled bottle. Desperately he reached down with a shaking hand and caught the thing by the neck. Using both hands to raise it he brought it to his lips and took a tentative swallow.

The liquor went down hard. It caught at the base of his throat, threatened to back up into the recesses of his mouth and, for the moment, he thought he'd lose the stuff. He worked his throat rapidly. The liquor managed to seep down into his belly in seconds, to bring a kind of warmth. Unsteadily he came to his feet. With widening eyes he stared around the place. She must have gone nuts! Everywhere he looked there was a mess, clothes, mud, junk. He reached for his wallet instinctively. It was still there.

Weakly he crossed to the bathroom door. He leaned forward and stared at his blotched and bloated features in the mirror. Goddam, he sure must've tied one on last night. He couldn't even remember where or when, how or why. Bewildered Harry came back to the room. He headed once again to the bedside, drawn to the bottle. Picking it up he stood weaving slightly, eyeing the amber liquid suspiciously as it sloshed back and forth in his shaking hands. If he could just get one more belt down, keep it down, he'd feel better. He had to get one slug in him; Christ, nobody could be like this and go on living.

Taking a deep breath Harry raised the bottle and tilted it against his lips. Again his throat muscles worked convulsively as he tried to retain the awful mouthful. This time it worked. The drink fought its way through, went down into the pit of his belly and started to spread along the frayed nerve network of his body, steadying the trembling, grounding him.

Turning, he once again surveyed the mess. He scowled at the sight of his best suit tossed around like that. By damn, she oughtn't to have done that; she knew goddam well better'n that. Tightening his lips he reached for the bottle, took one more hooker and then started picking up the stuff.

In the wake of the whisky reawakening came the anger, burning slow in the pit of his belly at first, smoldering, and then sparking into little hot flames that came up the walls of his insides, bringing the heat and smoke in his eyes, the thick, mottled color to his face. By God, who the hell did she think she was, raising cain all over the place like some pissed-off high school bitch! You wait, Harry raged, you wait 'til I get my hands on you, you'll get some goddam sense knocked into you!

When Harry had fought through washing, dressing and getting ready for the street, he looked for cigars. There were none. He fished out his wallet again. Suddenly stricken, he opened it and peered inside. The cash was still there! The bitch hadn't cleaned him out, too! With a grim smirk of satisfaction Harry opened the door to the hall and stepped out, pulling it shut with a soft click. She knew goddam well better than to touch anything that belonged to him! Why, if she ever took money from him he'd strangle her, kill her, that's what he'd do! And not think twice while doing it, either!

Harry moved down the street slowly. It was warmish and the effort stirred up his feverish blood and brought the perspiration slicking his forehead. What he wanted most was a cigar and this early in the morning there wouldn't be a drugstore open. Bitch! At the corner he stopped in surprise. The big drugstore on the next corner was lighted like a Christmas tree and he could even see people moving around inside.

Harry made the block in double time. He entered the store and went immediately to the tobacco counter, picked out six of his favorites and paid the girl. As she made change, he turned and surveyed the place incredulously. So many people, so early, he didn't get it!

"Sir?"

Her word brought him back and he accepted the change, looking at her as he did so. "You sure got a helluva lot of customers for first thing in the mornin', sister."

She was a washed-out blonde, tired, with bluish-black circles underscoring her milk-blue eyes. "You kiddin', mister," she asked wearily. "Mornin'? This here's Sunday night in my book!"

Harry paused in the act of cutting the cigar and stared at her. He licked his lips. "Sunday night!" he echoed.

"That's right." She leaned indolently on the counter and studied him for a long moment, then she rocked back on her heels and her mouth twisted in a derisive smirk. "Brother, you sure must've piled one on last night! Gees, you look like somethin' the cat dragged in!"

Harry went back outside and moved slowly along the sidewalk. Near the end of the building he stopped in close to the glass that was the drugstore wall and cupped his hands to light the cigar. As he puffed it to life, he took his hands down and looked into the store. The soda fountain stretched from front to back and, sitting alone, riffling through a magazine from the rack, was that big sonofabitch's friend, that Everett kid. He stood puffing the cigar to life, staring at Billy Joe Everett's back. Then he moved on up the block slowly. The thought of the big guy stabbed at his whisky-soaked brain. At the corner he stopped. He ran his hand over his scalp and scowled. There was something he couldn't quite remember; only he knew it had to do with that big bastard, that Troy Bannock, him and his free-running mouth.

Martha Devine glanced up from her place at the drive-in cash register and her face tightened. She watched Harry Marvel coming toward the main building, walking gingerly between the parked cars, almost mincing. He's had a few more, she realized irritably; he's been piling 'em on ever since last night. She took a deep breath and waited for him to come inside.

As he pulled open the big glass door and came in, Martha Devine knew she was wrong this time. True, he'd had a couple, nobody could doubt that. But he was sober. "What is it you're lookin' for, Harry?" she asked quietly, keeping her eyes on his mottled face.

"You know goddam well what I'm lookin' for," he snarled.

"Look, Harry, you and me don't want trouble. God knows you give us a bad enough time early this mornin'. You start somethin' now and I'm fixin' to call the police right off, I warn you!"

Harry stepped up close to her desk; his eyes were hard and cold. "Where is she?"

Martha Devine made a helpless gesture. "Harry, honest to God, I don't know where she is. She ain't here, I can tell you that. She didn't work yesterday; she ain't shown up for her shift tonight." She saw the dark color come flooding in his face and, despite her bravado, she knew she was afraid. "Harry, now look. I'm tellin' you the truth. Rita ain't been here. If she comes in, I'll tell her you been lookin' for her. I can't do nothin' more'n that."

His eyes left her and went to the little oblong serving slot between the kitchen and the restaurant. He swung on the pivot of his hips and surveyed the place, eyed each of the waitresses on duty carefully. His gaze came to the doors at the back of the place, the private ones for members of the staff.

"Harry!" Martha Devine anticipated his move. "She ain't here! She ain't here, Harry! I ain't hidin' her out from you, she just ain't here!" He was staring at her, suspicion sharp in his eyes. She kept herself under rigid control, keeping her voice low so the others in the place wouldn't know there was trouble.

"Harry, look," she pleaded. "Look, man, what's goin' on between you and Rita is your own damn business. I got a place to run and Rita's a damn good hop. I need good hops; I'm glad to get 'em. But what they do on their own time is their own business, Harry, and if you and Rita's had a fight or somethin', I'm sorry; only, it ain't gonna be where I'm doin' business." She paused, gulped for air and went on. "Harry, now look. I know you got a helluva temper and all and I reckon you and Rita has had some fights now and then. But that's your own business. I ain't about to hide her from you. I ain't interested in what you two do. She hops for me and that's it. Now, Harry, she ain't been inside this place for nearly forty-eight hours, and that's the God's truth. She didn't have to come in yesterday, that was her time off. I was expectin' her tonight and she ain't shown up and that makes me mad 'cause it puts me short-handed. But I'm tellin' you now straight, Harry, I'm gettin' sick and tired of you and her and all the trouble it's causin' and when she does show up I'm gonna can her. There's bad trouble walkin' with you, Harry, and we ain't got no room for it here."

"If she ..." Harry started.

Martha Devine cut him short. "No more, Harry, I don't want to hear no more. I said my piece. She ain't here and I want you should turn around and head straight out that door and, Harry, don't you come back, never. 'Cause if you do, I warn you, Harry, I'm gonna pick up this phone and call the cops and you're gonna find yourself in bad trouble." She collapsed like a pricked balloon. With one last reserve she pointed toward the double glass doors. "Okay, Harry, good-by!"

For a long time Harry Marvel stood balancing on the balls of his feet, regarding the woman across the counter with his little cold eyes. His lips had thinned down, were no more than an ugly slash across his face. If he had a retort to make, he made no attempt to do so. Jerking suddenly, he spun from the cashier's desk and butted the heavy glass door open with his palms and left.

Martha Devine trembled. She watched him make his way across the lot. Look at him, she raged, wrinkled suit, dirty shirt, needs a shave. And from the mud on his shoes you'd think he'd been out plowing all day!

# CHAPTER FOURTEEN

Will Bannock sat in his chair on the porch of the house and looked out over the fields. He was simply lazing, musing in the growing warmth of the ripening spring. Now and then his gaze followed a car or a truck and trailer rig as it went speeding along the highway; occasionally his eyes turned to the far-off field where Tom and Troy worked with the tractor, getting in the first plowing. The breeze from the west was gentle and unhurried, and there were times during the afternoon that Will's eyes closed for long moments. He dozed fitfully, only his ears alive, catching the sounds of Bess inside the house at her chores, the distant clatter of the machine, the breathless rush of an auto and the heightened roar of the trucks.

Tuned as he was to the multiple sounds around the place, Will caught the first hint of the automobile turning in the road from the highway. It brought his eyes open and, without changing position, he watched the approach of the car with narrowing eyes. The preacher, Joe Ben Potter's old sedan was carefully making its way toward the house.

Will scowled faintly and worked his mouth. He shifted irritably in his chair and tried to bring himself a little straighter.

The Reverend Joe Ben Potter brought his car up close to the front steps. For a moment he sat behind the wheel, letting the kicked-up dust settle, watching the dim, distant figures of the men working at their plowing. He dropped his eyes, examined the backs of his fingers as they clutched the round of the wheel.

Maybe he shouldn't be bothering about all this; maybe, sometimes, things was best left to work out as they would, in the Lord's way. It was difficult to know, sometimes. Yet, down deep inside him, he knew that he had had to come by, at least to speak his piece. He owed that to Will Bannock.

He stirred himself, opened the car door and stepped down, slamming it behind him. Coming around the rear of the machine he glanced up at Will sitting in his usual place, hunched up in that chair. The preacher hesitated; it occurred to him that it was hard to remember when Will Bannock hadn't been just sitting, letting the years slide past, just waiting.

"Howdy, Will," Joe Ben Potter said briskly.

"Howdy." Will still wore the look of scowling irritation. "Draw up a chair and set a spell," he invited grudgingly.

The preacher came to the top of the steps and looked down on the difficult member of his flock. "You feelin' peart today, Will?"

" 'Bout as peart as I reckon I ever will," Will snapped.

"You're lookin' fine, Will," Joe Ben Potter hastened, reaching for the straight-backed, weather-beaten chair, drawing it close to the other man.

"Shoot!" Will grunted. "Look like a cripple and know it." He eyed the preacher from under his scraggy brows.

" 'Pears to me you're gettin' all out of kilter with your callin' times, Potter," he commented dryly.

"A goodly lot of work to be done, Will," Joe Ben explained wearily.

"I reckon," said Will.

There was a little silence. The two men let their attentions wander across the field to where Tom and Troy were working under the hotting sun.

"Boys gettin' after the plowin', I reckon," Joe Ben observed.

"Weather's warmin' fast," Will observed. "Ground's gettin' in fair shape now."

Joe Ben raised his eyes and looked at the bank of thunderheads forming somewhere out west near the New Mexico border. "Radio says as how maybe there might could be some rain, come nightfall."

"We can use all we can get."

"Don't much care for this time of year," Joe Ben confessed. "Too much electricity in the air, too much wild weather."

Will had taken his eyes from the boys at work. He sat back a little more comfortably now and his gaze on his visitor narrowed. After a pause he swallowed and spoke, "You ain't payin' a call to talk about the weather, Joe Ben Potter."

The preacher contemplated him a little sadly. "It's somethin' I been thinkin' you ought to be knowin', Will."

"Somethin' like what?"

"Somethin' maybe concerns Troy."

Will Bannock felt the sudden quick shadow fall across his insides. He came forward a little in his chair and fixed the preacher's face with a sharp, worried look. "What is it about Troy, Potter?"

Joe Ben Potter brought his gaze to Will Bannock's lined face. He moistened his lips and kept his attention firmly riveted on the other man's eyes. "It's Martha who told me, last night, after she come back from town."

"Yeah?"

"Martha was doin' shoppin' … for the marryin' comin' up." Joe Ben colored faintly. At Will's impatient nod, that intense look still on his face, the preacher hurried on. "She was down at the big drugstore pickin' things up and she heard somebody talkin' the next aisle over, so she stops what she's doin' and listens, 'cause Troy's name come up and caught at her ears."

"Yeah?"

"There's a Godless, sinnin' man, Will, who's walkin' the streets of town sayin' things about Troy and some woman and how she's up and disappeared all of a sudden."

Will Bannock leaned forward precariously in the chair. His mouth had gone thin and there was a strained whiteness at the flanges of his nose. "What kind of talk's this from a preachin' man, Joe Ben Potter?" he rasped. "You got nothin' better to do than run around carryin' woman's crazy talkin' tales?"

"I know what you're thinkin', Will," Joe Ben shifted uncomfortably. "Only the man who's doin' the talkin' is a man a good many folks 'round these parts knows, Harry Marvel. He runs the skatin' rink in town, they tell me, and he's been sellin' whisky and beer to the youngsters and carryin' on a long time now with the woman."

"The woman," Will demanded in a hoarse whisper, "Who's the woman?"

"Flashy type woman, from what I been hearin', been workin' like a waitress 'round town, livin' with this man quite a spell, like man and wife. She's been missin' now maybe a week or so, never showed up for work and this here Marvel's been drinkin' heavy and talkin' about how Troy and her was cuttin' up nights."

Will Bannock released his hold on his twisted body. He lurched back against the chair, not taking his eyes from the unhappy preacher. His look had gone dark and there was the pulsing of the nerve in his cheek. "Who was doin' all this talkin'," his voice rose sharply, "who was shootin' off his goddam mouth 'bout my boy?"

Joe Ben Potter wet his lips and shifted nervously. "Martha got no look at 'em. By the time she was able to get 'round the aisle there was nobody in sight. They just up and cleared out."

"It's a lie, Potter!" Will smote the chair arm with his crippled hand. "It's a dirty, rotten, no-good, stinkin' lie!"

Helplessly the preacher shrugged. He splayed his hands in a supplicating gesture. "I reckon as how it was, Will. I just reckon as how you ought to be told what was bein' said, so's if you got to hearin' from somewheres else, it wouldn't come as no surprise to you, like to me."

"A lie, a lie, a no-good goddam lie!" Will chanted.

His sight went out over the fields and he stared at the tiny figures of the men at work.

"It ain't true, none of it, not about Troy, not my boy!"

Joe Ben Potter sat watching the older man compassionately. Will Bannock's great twisted hands worked convulsively, clasping and unclasping in agitation. His brain whirled. He wanted to get out there in the field, wanted to reach out and grab Troy's big shoulders, to shake him like a puppy until his teeth rattled, to force the truth to come spilling out of him right and honest. Yet, here he was, chained, robbed of manhood, fatherhood, helpless, no way left to do his duty. He turned and his mouth was ugly as he stared at the preacher who sat with head bowed.

"You told me what you come to tell me," Will's voice was chilled. "You got nothin' else to say, you best be goin' and leavin' me to handle my own."

When Joe Ben Potter raised his head, there was suffering in his eyes and compassion streaked on his face. "You had to know, Will," he said quietly. "You had to know what they was sayin' so's you'd be able to take care of your family when it comes. That's why I come. You had to know and I reckon as how I was the one had to tell you."

Something in Joe Ben Potter's simple manner, in his soft, quiet speech brought Will Bannock to a pause. He stared at this meek man, seeing all the things that stood out so open and naked on the face, and there came a little pricking of shame for the way he'd been acting. "I'm sorry," he choked. "I reckon as how none of it's your doin', none of it your fault. I spoke out rough and loud at you; it ain't your doin' and I'm obliged for what you done."

"I just reckoned you ought to know," Potter repeated simply.

"Yeah, 'course." Will waved his hand absently, his gaze going out again to the dust spiral in the field. "Yeah, I reckon I had to be hearin' sooner or later. Only," he swallowed with difficulty, "there ain't no truth in what that man's been sayin'; it's all a lie, a dirty, bad lie."

"I reckon so," Potter agreed slowly. "I'll be doin' a little prayin' that's the way it is."

Will's color had faded. The lines in his face were etched deeply and his eyes as they came back to the preacher were tired and there was a vague little shadow of hurt in them. "Yeah, preacher, you do that," he agreed softly, "you just keep on your prayin'. There's lots I ain't never cottoned to in your business; only, if there's any justice in Him at all, He ain't about to let a dirty, bad lie keep goin' 'round and 'round."

Joe Ben Potter flushed under the familiarity of Will Bannock's talk. Still, there was something in what he was saying. The preacher came to his feet and stood looking down on the gray crown of the farmer's head. "I reckon I best be goin' now," he said simply.

Will coughed lightly, raised his head and looked up into the other's face. "I reckon you done right and I'm mighty obliged to you for comin'," he said formally. His ears caught the sounds of Bess inside. "You … you want to be speakin' with the woman?"

Joe Ben Potter tried a slight smile. He reached down and touched the older man's shoulder. "Not this time, I reckon. Maybe it's best not."

"Maybe so, maybe so."

"God bless you, Will Bannock."

"Yeah," Will said.

He watched as the preacher went quickly down the steps, down the ragged walk to the car. In a moment car and preacher had gone, the car hidden behind the peacock plume of dust from the farm road. Will closed his eyes wearily. When he opened them the car had disappeared and the dust was settling back. It was then that he turned his head slowly, his gaze seeking them out in the field. He sat quietly now, looking at one of them, and he knew that all the fears he'd been having were coming home at last.

The sheriff sat back in his chair, tilted back, and stared across the little space at Harry Marvel. For a long time he'd hated Harry Marvel's guts, known what he was doing behind the screen of the skating rink, yet doing it so cleverly, openly yet secretly, that he'd never been able to get his hands on him. And now here he was, Harry Marvel, big shot, in a slopped-up shirt, baggy, wrinkled suit, unshaven, with blood-shot eyes, a mess after a ten-day drunk, trying to walk on two legs. With a heavy sigh the sheriff came forward, glanced around the room at the others, letting his look remain a fraction of a second on the newspaper reporter.

"Nothin' in the paper about this, Jim," he instructed absently.

He brought his attention back to Harry Marvel reluctantly. The man sat slumped, his big, reddish-patched hands clasped, his nails broken and dirty, fingers yellowed with nicotine stains, scarred with blisters from unfelt cigarette burns.

"So you don't know anything, Harry, that right? Don't know where she's gone to, don't know why? All you know is what you been shootin' off your mouth about around town, that she was layin' up with the kid, that she just up and poof! just like that!"

Harry Marvel brought his head up with an effort. Nothing made any sense any more. He squinted, trying to focus on the ballooning face across the desk top. "I don't know nothin'," he muttered huskily. "Just I know him and her was screwin' up a storm outside the rink and she ain't never come back since." Sudden animation sparked his reddened eyes and he stiffened sharply in the clutch of the chair. His eyes went wide and he looked around the room, met defiantly the stares of those watching him. "You ain't got no right holdin' me," he cried. "I ain't done nothin'."

"We're not holdin' you, Harry, not for anything more'n bein' drunk on the streets. That's the city's problem anyway. We're just askin', Harry, not holdin'."

"I don't know nothin' more'n I been sayin'." He slumped down and reached up to cradle his shaggy head in his big palms. "She's done gone, cleared out, and him, he knows...." He brought his eyes up, not changing his position, and he stared coldly into the sheriff's eyes. "You ask him what he done with her out there by the cars, you'll find out. I'm tellin' you he knows, by God!"

The disgust on the sheriff's face was marked. He glanced up at the man at his side. "You got this kid's name and everything?"

"Yeah, name's Bannock, Troy Bannock. Big bastard. Lives out maybe ten miles or so, lives with his family, farms."

The sheriff looked back at the prisoner. He chewed his lip thoughtfully. "Get rid of this bastard before I puke," he ordered softly. "He makes my guts sick."

"What you want done with him?"

"I don't give a damn what you do with him," the sheriff exploded. "Get him outta here, for Christ's sake. He's stinkin' up the place. Throw him back to the city, he's their baby anyway. Couple of days in the tank'll sober him up, maybe." The little note of regret crept into his voice. "Don't reckon we can hold a man for shootin' off his mouth, drunk or not," he spoke distinctly. "And, sometimes, drunks get to tellin' the truth, or some of it, at any rate."

They took Harry Marvel away then, stumbling and cursing at them, and silence and a kind of order seemed to come back to the office. The reporter sat back, nibbling almost daintily at the cuticle on his forefinger, his eyes busy. The officer still stood beside the desk. The sheriff sat with his eyes closed, and now he brought the palm of his hand down across his cheek. Without looking up at either of them, he spoke quietly.

"After the city got him, I called Martha Devine, runs that damn all-night drive-in. Marvel's been talkin' part truth, anyway. That dame of his never showed for work after that Saturday, never even got in touch, never has. Nobody's seen hide or hair of her since. Way I see it, Harry Marvel's a goddam fool; only, I don't reckon he's goddam fool enough to get rid of her and then go blabbin' all over town advertisin' the fact, drunk or sober." He paused and built a peaked tent with his fingers. "This Bannock guy. Maybe we ought to be havin' a talk with him. Devine says he's been hangin' 'round right enough. We'll do some talkin' 'round the rink, too. It'd piss me off good if it was so, but that drunk Marvel could be talkin' some truth through the bottom of the bottle." He laid his hands flat on the desk top and his eyes narrowed on the reporter watching him like that. "I got nothin' for your paper, not yet, see? When there's somethin', I'll tell you."

Will Bannock made his way torturedly across the flat of the yard between the house and the barn. He leaned heavily on his stick, his breathing hoarse with the effort of dragging the unwieldly, painful legs.

He'd watched from the porch until they had started in from the field, stayed there in his place until they neared the house.

And then he had hoisted himself from his chair, had gone through the house and watched them from the kitchen window until they had disappeared into the barn. It was then that he dragged himself on through the double doors to the back porch, down the precarious wooden steps to the uneven earth.

They both looked up startled when he pulled open the little door.

"Pa!" It was Tom who uttered the surprised exclamation. It had been a long time since Pa had tried the painful trip across the yard, a long time since he had even bothered to come around, to pay much attention to their work.

The old man did not reply. He very carefully closed the little door, stood looking at the two of them. "I got somethin' to say to Troy," he said finally. "Alone," he added quietly.

Tom flushed and shot an accusing glance at his brother. The little cleft was already deepening between Troy's brows as the frown moved in.

"Somethin' wrong, Pa?" he asked uneasily.

"Depends."

Pa had come close to the workbench. He stood there, propped by his stick, waiting, watching, while Tom snagged the oil rag from the counter and wiped the grease from his fingers. With a parting glance at his brother, Tom left them, going across the barn and out the door. Pa and Troy were alone in the old shed.

Pa made a move toward the bench and Troy anticipated him. Quickly he stepped ahead and caught up the wooden crate and brought it to his father. Grunting the old man eased himself down into sitting position, bringing his stick up between his legs. He leaned his weight on the support and eyed Troy speculatively.

"What's the matter, Pa? Somethin' wrong?" Troy asked again.

"Depends," his father said again.

Troy shifted uncomfortably before Pa's unwavering gaze. "I don't know what you're drivin' at, Pa."

"Then I'll be tellin' you," Will said shortly. "This afternoon while I was sittin' in that goddam chair on that goddam porch, that Joe Ben Potter comes by."

"Yeah?"

"Seems as though his woman's been shoppin' downtown for the marryin' stuff."

Troy shook his head and made a vague gesture. "I don't get it, Pa. What's Joe Ben Potter and Miz Dovely got to do with me?"

"I reckon he's been buttin' in," Will said hopefully. "Point is," he went on, "the preacher's woman hears somebody talkin' down in town and they's talkin' 'bout you."

" 'Bout me?"

"That's the fact." Will's gaze on his son's face sharpened. "They was two of 'em talkin' behind the stuff in the drugstore and they was sayin' as how there's a man named Harry somethin' who's been goin' 'round town talkin' about how you and some whorin' bitch of his has been carryin' on." Will paused and wet his lips. His eyes did not leave his son's face.

Something almost akin to relief burst in Troy. He turned away and shrugged elaborately. "Oh, her ... Rita." He turned back in a moment and looked directly at his father. "I been with her once, Pa, and that's the truth. It didn't mean nothin', just the once. It's all over and done with. You ought to know that, Pa, what with Nancy and all; it's over and done with."

Will Bannock leaned a little heavier on his stick and his eyes, stung with the lash of desperation, searched his son's face. "That ain't all there is to what Joe Ben Potter's been sayin', son."

"What then?"

"The woman's gone, disappeared. And that's the story this Harry's been talkin' in town."

Troy stared at his father. He moistened his lips nervously and turned away, running his hand over the blond spikes of his hair.

Will took a deep breath and forced himself to the question, his hands clenched tightly on the stick. "You know somethin' about this, Troy? I'm askin' you. You know somethin' about this here female up and disappearin'?"

Troy wheeled back, meeting his father's fearful eyes. "Christ, no, Pa, what're you thinkin'? I don't know nothin' about nobody disappearin'." He came close to Pa and he caught at his hands and clasped them tightly, hotly in front of him. "Pa, look, sure … I fooled around with her one night, didn't mean nothin', you know how it is. Next time I see her is the night Nance and me went skatin'." He stumbled to a pause and turned away, avoiding that pained look. "That night I see her. I got a bottle Billy Joe give me in the car. I ask her did she want a drink and she says yes. We went out and had a drink and that's all. We had it standin' right there out in the open, between the cars."

"That's all?"

Troy flushed and stared at his feet. "I reckon as how I tried makin' a pass, Pa, only she wouldn't. So I went back inside and got Nance and we left. I ain't seen her since, ain't even tried seein' her, don't want to see her."

There was an awful stillness inside the barn. Troy stood in front of his father, head bent, staring down. Pa leaned heavily on the stick and studied his son and inside him there was the unaccountable heavy weight of impending disaster.

"I believe you, son," Pa said eventually. He drew a long, unsteady breath. "I just wanted to hear from you … not the preacher, nobody else."

"I don't know nothin', Pa.…" Troy raised his stricken eyes.

"I reckon you don't if you say you don't. Only this here Harry reckons as how maybe you do." Pa hoisted himself to his feet and fought for balance. "Don't know this Harry, reckon as how I wouldn't much care to. Only I got me a feelin' he's spellin' trouble." He had started his shuffle across the earthen floor toward the door. He half turned, looking back to where his son stood. "We don't need trouble 'round here, we got plenty enough."

Troy followed his father. The warm late afternoon sun heated the yard, glanced its light off the board walls of the barn, bringing the sweat glistening on their brows. Off to the west the thunderheads piled themselves high against the sky and here and there jagged forks of lightning shot brilliant against the cloud black.

"Might could be we're gonna have us some rain," the old man mused. He hobbled toward the house, Troy trailing wearily in his wake. At the foot of the steps Will Bannock came to a halt and glanced up at the tight, drawn young face. "There ain't no need to go talkin' 'bout any of this to your Ma," he warned. "Leastways, not yet."

The sheriff sat, the officer stood at his side, the reporter kept nibbling at his cuticle, and all three eyed the big frightened blond boy. He had come in quietly when the officer had gone to the farm to bring him in; he'd come more bewildered than anything; he'd answered their questions, had told them his story, what there was to it, and now he sat there, dwarfing them even in his sitting, his big hands dangling between his legs, and he hadn't really told them anything at all.

There'd been the business of dragging Harry Marvel back from the city jail again; they'd had to sit through the stench of his presence and listen to his wild accusations against the boy, and they'd seen Troy Bannock and his sudden anger come spuming fast, had watched fascinated as those big hands had clenched into hammer fists and, in the mind of each of them, there had been the one, single truth ... if this one ever really let go, ever lost that quick-burning temper, ever struck out with those fists of his ... it was possible, all this, more than possible.

"Go over it again," the sheriff ordered shortly, leaning a little over the desk, the edge cutting into the swelling paunch. "Tell us about that night at the rink, about how you and her went out to the car and had a drink."

Troy swallowed and his eyes shifted from one face to the other in the close, hot room. "I told you just how it was, we just went out and had a drink, that's all."

"Just one drink apiece?" the sheriff asked, settling back, making that peaked tent with his thick, short fingers, never taking his eyes off the boy's pale face.

"Well, no ..." Troy flushed. "Two, maybe three, we killed the pint."

The little frown barely shadowed the sheriff's brow. "You said only a drink," he reminded.

"Well, I reckon I forgot."

There was a feeling glance between the sheriff and the officer and then the sheriff came up a little straighter in his chair. "Were you drunked up?" he demanded brusquely.

"No. No, we weren't drunk. Well ..." Troy confessed helplessly, "maybe we were feelin' a little, but," he hastened, "we weren't drunk."

"You forget whether it was one, two, three drinks out of the bottle." The sheriff's face tightened and he came forward. "Maybe you could be forgettin' other things, too, huh?"

"How you mean?" Troy wet his lips.

"You make a pass at the dame? Try and cop a feel maybe, somethin' like that?"

Again the deep flush darkened Troy's face. Again his glance whirled around the room before he spoke. "I reckon we fooled around some," he admitted low.

"Played with her tits maybe, got all steamed up ... maybe more?"

Troy made no answer. He swallowed painfully.

"Somethin' else." The sheriff spaced his words. "You ever screw this here Rita, like Harry says. You ever in her pants ... before this here Saturday night we been talkin' 'bout?"

Troy stared at his feet and nodded. "Once," he whispered.

The sheriff again shared a long glance with the officer. He sat back now and rebuilt the finger tent. Over the top of it he kept his eyes on Troy. "Maybe it's like this," he suggested quietly. "You had a piece once, you reckoned as how maybe you'd cut another one. This time she ain't havin' none. You have a few drinks, make a pass, fiddle around but she don't want no part of it. Bam! You slap her around and that's it." The sheriff came forward to the desk again. "Them are big hands you got there, boy. You got muscle and you got a temper, too, like when Harry Marvel was here." The sheriff laid his hands flat on the smooth desk top. "What'd you do with her, boy, huh? Where'd you hide her?"

The silence in the room was complete. The terror came sweeping over Troy. It felt as if the skin on his temples would burst with the rush of blood, that his throat had closed, cutting off breath from his lungs.

"No!" he cried, coming from the chair, looking frantically at the others. "I didn't do anything like that! He's lyin' to you, he's lyin' through his teeth! I don't know what happened to her, it's just like I told you.... Yeah, sure, I tried makin' a pass, only she wouldn't have none. Then I just left her there, right out on the parkin' lot, went back inside the rink. I haven't seen her since. I swear it, honest!"

The sheriff sat back and closed his eyes. It could be, he thought, it could be ... either way. "Sit down, boy," he ordered gruffly. "Don't be makin' so much noise. I gotta think."

The only sound in the place was the occasional jump of the minute hand on the electric clock. Sweat puddled on Troy, ridging through his pores, scumming his flesh, bringing the sickening musty smell of fear to his nostrils.

"I don't know," the sheriff confessed finally. He shoved the chair back and got to his feet. He walked around behind his man and paused close to the reporter. "Stop that goddam bitin' your nails, Jim, you make me jumpy as hell!" he barked.

After a long time the officer beside the desk cleared his throat. "What you want we should do with him?"

As if he had forgotten the officer and Troy, the sheriff stopped his pacing and stared in surprise. "Lock him up, I reckon," he sighed regretfully. "Just get him outta here, for Christ's sake, I gotta think." Turning away, his glance fell on the silent, gnawing reporter. "Jim," he warned ominously, "I'm askin' you as a favor, nothin' in the paper, not yet. I'll let you know." There was a grunt from the nibbler; the sheriff nodded sympathetically. "I know, only when this one breaks, it'll be a honey. You can wait. Meantime, I gotta think."

Harry Marvel stumbled out of the city jail cell on the third day and made his way back to the one-room apartment in a daze. In the three days in the cell by himself, Harry Marvel had not thought much about anything; the illness in him had been enough to cope with. The third day was warm, humid, and even at noon the clouds to the west were piling up over the rim of the city. There was a silence, oppressive and thick.

Harry climbed the stairs of the apartment house, moved wearily down the hall and shoved open the door to the room. Everything was as he had left it, the bed tangled and messy, sheets twisted and sweat-stained, blanket half on, half off the sagging mattress, pillows humped obscene and lumpy.

He moved to the dresser and stared in the drawer. The jumble inside was there, too.

He came back and sat down on the edge of the bed. He leaned forward, taking his head in his hands and closed his eyes. Nothing made any sense any more. There was no sense in her, just going off like that, just because of the big bastard. Harry groaned aloud and rocked back and forth, rolling on his fat buttocks. He wanted her; he wanted her so bad his gut ached. He needed her, needed her arms around him, her big breasts soft and hot against his naked chest, needed her strong, long legs catching him, needed the dark, warm knowing of her.

He straightened and stared across the room with sightless eyes. His lips thinned down and the line of his jaw hardened tightly. He had no right doing what he done to her, no matter what, the big sonofabitch! He had no right touching Rita, no matter what!

Harry came to his feet and ran his sweating palms down the sides of his wrinkled trousers. Now he remembered some of it; he remembered how it had been that night at the rink, how he'd seen the two of them heading out in the dark, seen them standing there close, seen the arch of the big back bent over her in the shadows.

Now he remembered the last few days, the sonsofbitches in the police station talking, talking, talking, getting nowhere until he told 'em what was what. By God, Harry Marvel told 'em what they wanted to know.

He began to pace in the half-lit room, cutting across the thin beam of sunlight that forced into the room through the tattered shade. Back and forth, back and forth. He'd told 'em. By God, he'd told 'em and told 'em plenty. He'd told 'em how it was the last time he'd seen her, out there whorin' with that big fellow, and how that was the last goddam time he'd ever seen her!

Harry stopped short in the center of the cheap room and pulled himself straight. They'd believed him, too, them no-good copper sonsofbitches. They'd listened to what he had to say and then they'd come and got him and dragged him over there to put the finger on the bastard. He knew 'cause hadn't they let him go and hung onto that kid? He'd seen the bastard with his own eyes, sitting there all hunched over, with the three of 'em in the room, just like before, asking all them goddam questions, and him, not so goddam cocky any more, with his head down and his hands locked down between his legs.

That's the way it should be. Harry whispered to the silent room, anybody does somethin' to Rita gets his ass in a jam. Nobody got away with anything when Harry Marvel was around, by God! He'd told 'em and they'd listened and they'd gone out and picked him up and now it was his ass in a sling, by God! The trembling, the excited, fever-rising tremoring, took hold of Harry Marvel and he clenched his fists to try and hold it down, to push it aside. By God, they got him now and his ass was cooked. You start screwin' around Harry Marvel, only it's you gets screwed, brother, and no kissin'.

It was Cressy's idea, all her own. They all sat there in the parlor, Pa and Ma, Joe Ben Potter and Martha Dovely and Tom and her, all sitting there as if it were a funeral or something. Sure, it had been a shock when the policeman had come and taken Troy off with him; sure, they were sick and helpless and didn't know what to do next. Joe Ben Potter was the preacher; it was only right he came along when he heard. Maybe he could help somehow, she didn't know much about that. Only there was something to do, she knew, and she'd been sitting among them trying to work through the confusion in her mind to think what it was. And now she knew. Outside the thunder was heavy and the wind was strong and there was the splattering of rain on the roof and against the windows.

"Tom," she spoke up suddenly, "I gotta have the keys to the car, any car."

He glanced up at her, then looked at the windows, at the storm-swept twilight. "You can't go drivin' off with the weather like this!"

She came to his side, knowing that their eyes were on every move she made. "Tom, please, give me the keys," she repeated urgently. She turned away and went to the hall. "I'll get my coat."

He watched her go and then he looked at his parents, at the sharply-etched concern on their faces. "She's goin' to town," he told them dully. There was no reaction in them. The old man looked as if he was ill; the mother's face was twisted, hurt, uncomprehending. There was no help here. Tom struggled to his feet and followed his wife down the hall. He watched from the doorway as she worked feverishly into the coat and picked up her purse from the dresser.

"What the hell you up to?"

"I'm gonna try and see Troy, somebody ought."

"They won't let you."

"Maybe." She set her lips firm. She came up close to him and held out her hand. "The keys."

"My God, Cressy, you gone nuts? You can't go out in this; it's stormin' like the devil!"

"I been through storms before. It'll be over before you know it. This ain't nothin'."

"You can't go."

Her eyes flashed. "I'm goin'." The statement was flat, final and he knew it. There was a hard, determined look in her face that he'd never seen there before.

"I'll drive you, if you're so all-fired hot to go."

She laid her hand on his arm and her manner softened. "They'll need you here, Tom. You gotta stay. I'll be okay, honey. Listen, it's lettin' up already."

Both of them cocked their heads and knew she was lying. The storm was at its peak and the wind howled around the eaves of the old house, pulling and tearing and battering.

"Tom?" Her pressure increased.

"It's a damn fool idea," he protested angrily. "There ain't nothin' you can do, goin' all that way. There ain't nothin' nobody can do 'til mornin'."

"There's somethin' I can do and I'm gonna do it. I owe it to Troy to try." She held his arm in a tight grip. "The keys, Tom," she repeated.

Automatically he reached into his pocket and brought out the chain of keys. He detached the car key and gave it to her. She took it and then stood on tiptoe and kissed him.

"Don't go frettin' 'round them," she warned. "They got enough now without that." She patted his hand, much as she might pat the hand of a worried child. "I'll be okay. I won't be late."

With that she moved around him and was gone. He turned and saw the flick of her skirt as she disappeared into the kitchen, heard the opening and closing of the two back doors, and then there was nothing but the crashing of the storm outside, the brilliant explosions of lightning flashes in the window. Only dimly could he hear the car start; only momentarily did he catch sight of the headlights as she passed by the house, headed for the highway and town. Slowly, the frown deep on his brow, he started back down the hall to where they sat and, as he came near, he could hear Joe Ben Potter's voice low, and he was praying.

The worst of the storm had passed by the time Cressy had reached town. She drove into a gas station, looked up the street address in the phone book, and then cut across town, driving carefully through rain-flooded streets, knowing where she was going and what she was going to do.

It took only a pause before Herbert Collins answered the chime and opened the door and faced her.

"I'm Cressy Bannock," she said without preamble. "Tom Bannock's wife, Troy's sister-in-law."

Herbert Collins stared at her, then caught himself and stepped inside. "It's terrible," he blurted as she swept past him. "They let him call Nancy earlier. There's some terrible mistake, I know there's been a mistake."

She flashed him a sharp glance as she entered the little hall, then found herself in the wide opening to the living room. The woman she judged must be Mrs. Collins was seated in the chair on the right of the room and the face that was turned up to Cressy's glance was tear-marked.

"You're Mrs. Collins," Cressy said, advancing. "I'm Troy's sister-in-law."

Mrs. Collins's tears began to rise again, silvering her eyes. "It's so awful," she choked. "So unexpected and all that publicity."

Cressy stood looking down at her without sympathy. She was barely aware that Herbert Collins had followed her into the room, had come up alongside her and was standing there helplessly, looking down pityingly on his shattered wife.

"I want to see Nancy," Cressy demanded bluntly.

Mrs. Collins dabbed at her eyes and tried to gain control. "She ... she's upstairs in her room; she doesn't want to see anybody, not even us."

Cressy's voice came evenly. "Doesn't she even want to see Troy?"

"Troy?" Mrs. Collins took down the handkerchief and stared at her. "But he's in jail! He said he was in jail, she can't see him!"

"I think maybe she can, Mrs. Collins," Cressy said quietly. "Least, it's worth a try, isn't it?" There was no response from the woman in the chair. "You see, Mrs. Collins, it's now Troy needs her; perhaps it's the first time he's ever needed anyone, really."

Herbert Collins spoke up then, spoke suddenly, and his voice took on an unaccustomed authority. "I think maybe she's right; it's worth a try. Maybe both of them need each other. I'll get my coat," he said to Cressy.

"No ..." Cressy stayed him with her hand. "No ... not this time, just Nancy and me." She hesitated. "You see, he needs family now, way I see it, those who believe."

Herbert Collins stayed as he was. He stared at this young woman who held him. Now he saw her as she was for the first time, young and determined and he knew what she meant. He moved past her, turned at the doorway. "I'll tell her you're waiting," he said.

There was a long silence after he had gone upstairs. Mrs. Collins finished with the weeping and blew her nose lustily. She shot a tentative glance at the young woman who stood solidly, her hands thrust deep in the pockets of the tan raincoat. "How could it have happened?" Mrs. Collins asked plaintively. "Troy's such a nice boy."

Cressy's eyes were cool. "It's the nice boys who make mistakes sometimes," she observed.

Fear spiraled in Mrs. Collins's eyes and she half rose from the chair. "You ... you don't think he had anything to do with this woman?"

"With the woman ... as a woman, yes," Cressy said flatly. "With her disappearin' like that, no." She stared down on the older woman and she saw her for what she was and her eyes softened. Her voice came low. "Troy's a young, healthy man, Mrs. Collins, and he's all man. Sure, I guess he played around; only, it's never really meant anything, not until now. Troy's been livin' from day to day, Mrs. Collins." She came closer and her fingertips reached down and touched Mrs. Collins's shoulder. "Troy talked to me the night him and Nancy got engaged. Troy's found what he wants and it's a whole lifetime, not day to day any more."

There was a stir at the doorway and Herbert Collins came into the room followed by his daughter. For a moment Cressy and Nancy's eyes met and held and then there was a thin smile that touched Nancy's lips.

"Hello, Cressy," she said softly.

"Hello, Nancy."

She's a woman already, Cressy thought. She suddenly remembered the only other time she'd seen her, met her downtown in the drugstore with Troy and she'd thought then that this was a mere girl, a child, lovely and sweet, but a child. Now she was a woman, still lovely, still young, but Troy's mistake had forced sudden womanhood on her.

"Shall we get goin'?" Cressy urged, going to the door.

Nancy crossed the room, leaned down and kissed her mother's cheek. She straightened and glanced at her father's worried face. "We probably won't be too long," she said firmly. "I must see him, if I can, Daddy."

Herbert Collins merely nodded. He watched the two young women as they left the room. "She has strength, that Mrs. Bannock," he commented briefly. "Come to think of it, they both have."

Cressy had little difficulty in achieving her wish. The officer in charge had explained that it was irregular and all that, but, as he looked at the young women with the serious eyes, as he thought of that poor kid upstairs who sat on the cell bunk with that hopelessness in his eyes hour after hour, he decided the hell with it. He gave them ten minutes.

Cressy entered the cell first. She came in and looked down at him and then she was crouching at his side. Taking his hands down from his worn face, she kissed him gently on the cheek. "Don't you fret, Troy," she crooned. "We know, all of us know the truth. Somebody's made a mistake, a terrible mistake, but it'll come out all right."

"You were good to come, Cressy, the storm and all." He looked beyond her, searching. "You come alone?"

"It wasn't right, the others comin', not tonight. They'll come later. They're all right; Tom's stayin' with them and Joe Ben Potter's there, too."

He looked down into her eyes and his face was drawn and sober. "Tell 'em ... tell Pa I don't know what happened to her. I swear before God I don't know nothin'!"

"We know that, Troy. We've known that all along. It'll work out all right."

She remembered the time and got to her feet stiffly. "I'm not alone, Troy," she said, bringing her eyes to him. The faint smile came to her lips. She turned and went to the door and beckoned. In a moment Nancy was there, tears in her eyes, her lips trembling slightly.

Troy came to his feet and plunged across to her, sweeping her into the protecting circle of his big arms, bringing her close and hard against him. Cressy left them alone, the lump in her throat as big as a watermelon.

Nancy wept, burying her face against his chest, clutching at him with desperate fingers. "I ... I said I wouldn't," she wailed. "I wasn't gonna do this!"

His face was buried in her hair and he kissed her repeatedly. "I'm sorry, honey, I'm so sorry," he kept saying over and over again.

Nancy thrust herself from him, backed away so that she could look up into his face. "She wasn't any good, Troy, she never was any good, never! Now she's gone and lost herself and it's you she's got in trouble! She's bad, Troy, bad through!"

His eyes were troubled. "She isn't bad, Nance, not really. She's just … Rita, that's all. She'll turn up somehow; she'll come back. Then it'll be over and done with; then there'll be just us, you and me, no more Ritas, no more trouble."

She came to him and clung to him, as if she feared ever to let him go from her again. "I'm afraid, Troy," she whispered. "I'm afraid for us."

He thrust her from him, held her firmly at arms' length. "We can't be afraid, Nance," he warned. "We mustn't be scared. Now they don't know what happened to her, but somebody's seen her; she can't just have gone up in smoke! Billy Joe saw her that night; lots of others must have seen her down at the rink, at the drive-in. They know; they'll tell the truth."

Nancy moved out of his hold and her eyes were wide on him. "You don't know," she whispered. "You don't know, do you?"

"Know what?" he asked, the fear waving over him in spite of his will.

"The paper, Troy, the radio, TV. They've been tellin' about it all day. They haven't mentioned you but they've been asking everybody, only nobody remembers; nobody can remember seeing her after you went outside with her."

Troy collapsed on the edge of the bunk and stared at her. He wet his lips. "Even Billy Joe?" he asked huskily.

She came to his side, knelt by him, gripping his thigh with her hot fingers. "Billy Joe told the truth, Troy, he just didn't see her. Nobody was paying attention, Troy; it was crowded, remember? They tell the truth, but they didn't see her." Her voice broke and she laid her cheek against his leg and fought to keep the tears back.

"Oh, my Jesus!" Troy groaned. "I was countin' on that, hopin', prayin' even."

Nancy gained her control. She rose to her feet and looked down on him tenderly. "There is truth, Troy," she said quietly. "Somebody knows ... God knows. He'll see it comes out right." She bent down and took his head in her hands and kissed him full on the lips. "Don't you worry, honey, don't doubt," she encouraged. "I'll find the truth, somebody will. She's not so far away. Maybe she'll read about it and come back and clear the whole thing up."

"Nancy?" Cressy's interruption was gentle. "We gotta go now."

Nancy straightened and smiled tremulously at the other woman. "All right, I understand." She looked back at Troy. "I love you, Troy," she said simply. "I'll always love you because you're right and clean and honest. I want my life with you and nobody, no Rita, can take that away from me or from you, remember that." She bent down and kissed him quickly and before he could reach up for her she was gone.

Troy looked around the clean, bare walls of the cell. This was what they meant by loneliness, he thought, just being alone, not knowing, not being able to be with those you loved, caring so much, wanting so much. He brought his feet up and stretched out full-length on the bunk, turning his face to the wall, and began his waiting.

# CHAPTER FIFTEEN

They kept the reporters outside this time, including Jim, the cuticle-nibbler, banished now for all time from the police beat for leaking the story. They had something to tell Troy and what they were going to say was neither for the public ear nor pleasant.

The sheriff sat back, fingers peaked, and the officer stood as before at his side. There were others now, the county district attorney, looking pleasant but determined, and a secretary who worked silently on a stenotype.

They brought Troy into the office and sat him in the same chair where he had been seated before.

The sheriff eyed him a long time before he spoke. The boy looked beat, tired out; his eyes were red-rimmed, bloodshot, and his nerves were edgy; his manner was openly defensive.

"You get to see your folks yesterday?" the sheriff asked kindly. "Have a good visit?"

The knob in Troy's throat came sudden and huge, blocking away speech, cutting short his wind. Yeah, he nodded, he'd seen 'em, Tom trying to be reassuring and looking sick, Pa sad and unsure and pressuring his shoulder with a squeeze of his gnarled hand, Ma crying softly into her handkerchief and trying not to let him see, and Cressy, quiet, strong, only her eyes speaking to him.

"Your Daddy's a fine man," the sheriff was saying. "Known him a long time now. Tough break he's had with that arthritis."

The sheriff came forward and picked up the fattening file before him. "Son," he said slowly, deliberately, "we done like we said we was gonna do. We been askin' everybody we could find who was at the rink that night. We been askin' everybody we could lay our hands on. Nobody makes much sense." He riffled the papers, searching for something. "Oh, yeah, here it is. Friend of yours, Billy Joe Everett?" He waited for Troy's slight nod, saw the surprise and hope come springing into the young eyes, saw the quick moistening of the lips. "We been talkin' to young Everett, talkin' quite a bit, kind of refreshin' his memory, you might say."

Troy closed his eyes, trying to think back to what Billy Joe could know about Rita and him, other than what the rest already knew. What had he said to Billy Joe? The sheriff's voice cut across his thinking.

"Accordin' to this Everett boy, you and him had some talk about Rita that night there at the rink."

Now he remembered. He remembered the whisky bottle and how Billy Joe had twigged on to where his own bottle had gone so fast, how they'd gone out there and had a drink from Billy Joe's bottle afterward. Dumbly he nodded.

The sheriff continued his perusal. "Accordin' to Everett, later on you come 'round askin' if he seen Rita Karnes, after you told him you'd been outside drinkin' with her." He looked up, waited for Troy's nod. Troy nodded.

"Everett says he warned you not to go foolin' with Rita, that she was Marvel's girl, that you ought to stay with what you had, this little Collins kid you're engaged to."

It was true, all of it was true. It sounded so cheap, so dirty. Troy closed his eyes, feeling the sweat starting to ooze down his spine, across his forehead, in the palms of his hands.

"Then you had some words with Harry Marvel at the door and left the rink, right?"

"Yes, sir."

"You took the girl, the Collins girl, for a ride and then on home ... That's the night you got engaged, right?"

"Yes ... yes, sir."

"Only, this is funny ..." The sheriff's voice had hardened and his eyes turned cool and remote. Without referring to the file, he droned on. "... After you took the Collins kid home, you doubled back to the drive-in where Rita works. You park the car and go on inside and order a hamburger. Everett comes up and the two of you shoot the breeze. You tell him about gettin' engaged and all, only you don't look like you was too happy about it, look kinda tired and all, like you had a hard night. Everett starts back to join his friends in the booth and suddenly you call him back. You make a point of askin' about Rita again, ask if she'd come around the rink after you and the Collins kid left, right?"

"Yes, sir, that's right, only, I ... you see, I wanted to make sure she wouldn't cause no trouble...." Troy's voice trailed off.

"There ain't much more." The sheriff disregarded Troy's attempt. "You ask if Rita showed. Everett says no. He asks you then how come you're so all-fired interested in why she shows or not, if you was chasin' after her again. You say, no, nothin' important, that you was ... lemme see here ... 'just askin' ' "

The sickness inside Troy had started the size of a droplet and had come slowly, spreading like thick molasses, coming up over him, bringing the sweat out, filling up through him until he wanted to lean over and retch, cleanse himself of the ugly mess inside.

The sheriff had stopped. He waved his hand casually. "There's some more," he confided almost intimately. "We heard about how you and your brother fought over somethin', how you got a helluva temper and lose your head now and then when you don't get your way, all that crap." There was a pause. "Point is, boy, there ain't no way of tellin' what's right and what's wrong from all this." He waved his hand at the file. "Only thing we know for sure is you was apparently the last one with her; she's gone and you got a story that's got more holes than swiss cheese, son, and that's about it."

Troy slumped forward in despair, his shoulders rounded, and his eyes dull on the bland face of the man across the desk. What more could he say, other than what had already been said? How could he say his only mistake had been fooling around, nothing more than that? What about the others who knew her? How come they went scot free and here he was with them trying to pin her running away on him?

"Tell you what we're gonna do, son." The sheriff had come forward again, had laid his hands on the desk, covering the file, and his voice had resumed its quiet, persuasive tone. "Looks like you and me are gonna take a little ride."

Troy's brows rose. Ride? The terror came exploding in his middle and he flashed a wild glance at the other, the impassive faces in the room. "Ride, sir?" he echoed weakly.

In that confidential, smooth way, the sheriff went on. "Down at Austin they got a machine that's a whiz, son. You probably heard about it. Call it by some fancy name, but most of us call it a lie detector."

The silence in the room was taut and brittle. Lie detector, Troy thought, they wanted him to tell his story all over again so that machine with its graphs and its needle would listen and mark down the rights and the wrongs and if the score was wrong at the end.... Oh, my God!

" 'Course, you got to co-operate. If what you been sayin' is all true, then no sweat. 'Course, if it isn't ..." The sheriff sat back and let his words go floating off in the stillness of the room. "Well, son?" he asked at last.

"Yeah … sure," Troy agreed huskily. "Anything …"

The sheriff smiled. He sat straight and rubbed his hands together, like a businessman who has concluded the deal. "Good boy!" He glanced up at his assistant. "Call 'em down in Austin, Ray. Tell 'em we leave in the morning. Tell 'em, well … just tell 'em to have everything set up."

It was cloudy and humid when they left town the next morning. The skies were dark and ominous, and, as they drove out of town and started on the hundreds of miles of open country, the sheriff eyed the heavens critically.

"Sure as hell hate travelin' in twister weather," he remarked gruffly. "Ought to be stayin' home case one of them goddam things touches down 'round here." He glanced at the young man at his side, down at the hands loose in the lap, clasped between the two powerful thighs. There were no handcuffs; the sheriff couldn't bring himself to shackle Will Bannock's boy, no matter what.

"Had a couple last night up near Gross Corners," Ray said from the back seat.

"Couple of what?"

"Twisters." Ray paused and stared out over the passing fields. "Nothin' happened. One touched a couple of times, didn't get nothin'. Other one never touched down, I reckon."

The sheriff drove fast and sure. "Sure as hell remember that one at Silverton couple of years back. Took the whole goddam town off the map." He glanced at Troy who was keeping his eyes on the straight road ahead. "I tell you, son, there wasn't nothin' left but matchsticks when that one got through with some of them places."

"Good day for 'em today all right," Ray remarked, eyeing the troubled skies distastefully.

"Reckon there'll be a couple somewheres along the way," the sheriff agreed amiably.

The ride went on and on. The business at Austin was over and done with in the space of time it would have taken them to drive twenty-five miles. After it was over they got in the car and came back to the plains, driving through the pitch-black night, through clear skies, through thunder, lightning, hail once, and back into muddy skies.

Troy was exhausted. He sat in back with Ray on the return trip and laid his head against the back of the seat, his eyes closed, and tried not to think about what was happening to him—the whole, weird, incredible, awful joke that had come to rest on his shoulders.

The lie-detector test had gone off smoothly enough. He'd told the whole story all over again, had answered their questions, then sat alone in a guarded room while they went off somewhere else and did whatever they had to do.

When the sheriff had come back to get him, he carried the folder under his arm and there was a sober look on his face. He had come to the door, had stood there for a long moment, just looking down on him speculatively, then he had sighed and motioned. "Come on, son," he had said quietly, wearily. "Reckon we best be hittin' the road home. Got some twisters actin' up 'round there and that's where we belong."

None of them spoke on the ride back. None of them made reference to the results of the test. The folder lay on the seat next to the sheriff up front and it rode along with them, its secret inside, the flap tied down with a little washer-like seal and the string wound around it.

Troy had no feeling about any of it any more. He was tired and beat. He'd told the story so many times now, he wasn't sure if he told it the right way or the wrong. All he knew was he'd tried to tell the truth, tried to remember everything as it had happened that awful night and even the time before. Now he didn't care; everything was done. They could do whatever they wanted with the results of the test, with him. All he wanted was to be left alone.

Lying there, his head bouncing on the back of the seat, he tried to call up the faces of Nancy, of Pa and Ma, of Tom and Cressy. Nothing would come. All of them seemed so far away, so remote, in some other world, almost as if he had never known them, lived with them, loved them. He was here and he was alone.

Sleep came over him. It drew a deep, black velvet curtain over him, as the sheet is drawn over the face of a man dead, and he slept. He slept in a dark, empty void, dreamless, formless, without feeling.

He woke only once. They had pulled into a service station for gas and he stirred and opened his eyes, not changing his position. Surprised, he noticed they had left him alone in the car, were standing at the side, talking together in low tones, the sheriff and deputy. For a mad moment Troy thought wildly of escape. Even then the ironic twist caught his lips. Get away to where? Across the vast, far-flung limitless stretch of West Texas and the whole world on foot?

"Don't look so hot tonight," he heard the sheriff say.

"Gonna be a mean couple of hours," Ray agreed.

He peered out. They were standing together, both staring at the sky, at the low scudding, swirling clouds that came rushing from the south. The sheriff picked at his teeth worriedly with a matchstick and finally he shrugged.

"Best get back to town quick as we can; never should have left." He flipped the match across the graveled station drive. "Sure as hell gonna be a nest of twisters turned loose tonight!"

# CHAPTER SIXTEEN

The sheriff was right. By the time the car reached the county jail, by the time Troy had been taken to his cell, the tornado alert had been sounded. The disaster lurked above the city in the boiling bowels of the ugly, swollen clouds that pressed over the area.

Radio announcers broke into programs announcing the alert, tracing the passages of minor twisters over the area; television news rooms cut off national programs to brief the local viewers on the areas of possible terror and destruction. At the newspaper the short-wave radio kept picking up police-car messages, raucous and scratching, as the various units headed for vantage points to keep an eye on the capricious skies; while newsmen climbed to the roof of the building to peer apprehensively into the murk beyond the downtown area for the first sign of danger.

On the roof of the county jail the sheriff and his deputy, Ray, watched the turbulent, seething mass of bruise-black clouds, binoculars in hand, keeping their attention riveted to the pulsing mass. All thoughts of a woman named Rita Karnes were banished in the common threat.

Suddenly the deputy stiffened. He raised his glasses quickly toward the southwest and focused them on the big, black, wicked-looking cloud that hung a mile or so beyond the outskirts of the city, For a little eternity he stared through the magnifying circle of the glass, watching intently, making sure. Then, without taking his glasses down, he groped for the man at his side and pointed with the same hand. Together the two men watched.

"Sure to God is!" the sheriff muttered. "She's comin' down sure as hell!"

The cloud was enormous; it dwarfed the earth beneath. It had gathered itself into a festering, evil bank, hung low to the earth, and now, as the two men stared in horror, they could see the throbbing, pulsing teat that had burst through like a rupture on the boiling loin of the massing formation.

The teat thrust down out of the cloud like a swollen finger, distended and ugly, wavering only slightly now, back and forth, as if it were loose and dangling without direction or purpose.

As the men watched, the pustule began to grow, to come reaching down, and, as the thinning teat came forth, it moved back from its source, arcing with evil grace, curving down, sucking down swiftly, hungrily seeking the earth, its great spinning famished mouth drawn starved to the spoils of the land.

"Jesus Christ!" the sheriff moaned. "It's a heller!"

"She headin' this way?" Ray cried. "I can't tell, is she headin' this way?"

"Can't make out," the sheriff yelled.

They stared, transfixed. Every instinct told them to abandon the roof, to flee below, to seek out a shelter against the vortex of death that had begun to waver and move swiftly in its south to northeast course. From the rooftops of the city now watchers could see the thing's base, catch an occasional glimpse of flying debris as it spun from the funnel at the point of smashing contact. It traveled swiftly, its racing mouth sucking eagerly along the path, churning, demolishing trees, any obstacle in the way, with the fascinating, almost ludicrous look of a giant egg-beater at work.

"Not comin' this way, thank God!" the sheriff shouted. "Headin' outside town, headin' out country!"

It was true. The thing, now a thin, horrible pencil curve against the sky, was headed northeast, heading out toward the open farm land to the west of town. They saw the funnel lift suddenly, as if it had been recalled by some enormous winch hidden in the parent cloud. The funnel lifted and hung, dangling idiotically midway between cloud and earth, impotent, lifeless. The tornado hurried past the awe-stricken eyes of the city, a hanging sword of Damocles threat headed now for the scattered, luckless farms and the open land.

As the tornado skirted the edge of town, the mouth came down once more for a last taste of earth. The men watched as it moved from them, was caught up again in the swift rush of cloud, retracting up into the formless mass that had spawned it. As quickly as it had come, it had gone on its way. The city had been spared this time; only the scattered buildings in the open country were hit with the impact of the sucking monster.

The sheriff took down his glasses. "That was a bastard," he grunted. "We can do without too goddam many of them."

Ray was shaken. "There's times I say to myself I'm gettin' the hell outta this part of the country. Every spring's the same; every year I get the hell scared outta me!"

The sheriff smiled thinly. "There's a couple of hundred thousand people round these here parts been thinkin' the same thing year after year. Only"—he grinned—"we don't go nowheres else; we sit around waitin' for the next one, always hopin' it ain't gonna be us that gets it."

Downstairs they picked up the first reports. There was no appreciable damage. It'd got a couple of barns, a fence or two, farm buildings of one kind or another. Nobody reported dead or even injured, luckily. The sheriff finished the report, glanced at the area map on the wall. Here and there were little tornado cut-outs stuck to regions where twisters had been reported. He counted seven.

"By God, we're gettin' off lucky," he breathed. "Seven of the bastards and nobody hurt yet. Maybe all this damn alert stuff pays off at that!"

Later that night the storm passed on its way. The alert was lifted after a heavy downpour, scattered hail over the area, and some high winds. Three hours later the sky was full of new-washed, enigmatic stars whose very twinkling belied the horror that had cut them from view temporarily. Violence had come and had gone. The countryside slept its exhausted grateful sleep.

# CHAPTER SEVENTEEN

Haggard, drawn after the long ride to Austin and back, plus the fearful night hours, the sheriff sat at his desk, blinking his eyes, trying to rid them of the irritating scratch that blurred everything he looked at. He was poking at the bits of cloth piled on his desk, the slacks, the blouse, the women's panties, the stockings, the pair of high-heeled shoes. He raised his eyes and blinked again. The man standing in front of him was middle-aged, in khaki shirt and worn levis. He stood uneasily, twisting a sweat-stained hat, turning it by the brim, working it with work-scarred, heavy, blunt-nailed hands. The sheriff turned and eyed the man at the farmer's side. This was the preacher, name Joe Ben Potter, Reverend, that is. He brought his attention back to the nervous farmer.

"You say you farm west of town? How far?"

The farmer shrugged. " 'Bout five, six miles, never rightly counted 'em off."

"Out by the old gin?"

"Yes, sir."

"You mind tellin' me all over again?" The sheriff smiled thinly. "I had me a lousy night."

"Well, like I told the preacher here, I been readyin' the field the past couple of weeks, ever since the weather turned fair. You see, sir, I rent the place, it ain't really mine ... and so I get out there first thing this mornin', want to keep at the plowin' steady so's I can plant soon as the ground's dry enough."

The sheriff toyed with the pencil and made little circles on the pad that bore the man's name, Bob Ryan, and that of Joe Ben Potter. "How come you was plowin' this mornin'? Way I heard tell everything Was rained out last night."

"No, sir. It rained all over hell and gone but she sure didn't wet down my section. Missed the place complete."

This wasn't unusual; peculiar weather was the trademark of the area. One man's place would be flooded or hailed out; the next man could lie parched for a drop and never see a puddle.

"Go on."

"Well, sir, like I told Mr. Potter here, I got goin' right early, reckoned as how I'd get workin' so long as the weather held good. I been plowin' along the line the past few days, reckoned as how I'd edge her first and work toward center." The man paused, gulped and stared down at his battered hat. "That's how I come on this stuff."

"How?"

"Well." The man raised his head and his eyes with the milky blue whites wet in the weather-beaten brown of his face rested squarely on the sheriff. "I been workin' along this line, like I been sayin', only there's a set of damn posts there so's I can't work in to the very edge. I gotta let maybe a foot go, maybe two or three some places, else I'd be rammin' them posts every time. Lady ownin' the place, she told me clear she don't want none of them posts outta there, if'n I crack one of 'em—and I do sometimes—I gotta put 'em back, so's I steer clear most times, wide clear."

"Tornado last night, got that old gin, didn't it?" the sheriff asked suddenly.

"Hell, yes, sir, smashed the old place to bits. Ain't nothin' left out there but kindlin' wood this mornin'."

"Go on with what you were sayin'."

The farmer cleared his throat noisily. "Well, sir, like I said, I come workin' the cat along the row this mornin', stoppin' every now and then to clear away some of that old gin what blowed all across the section, when, all of a sudden, like I says to Mr. Potter here, there's this piece of stuff wrapped around one of them pesky posts."

"Which piece of stuff?"

"That one there, the pants." The farmer colored, bent forward and pointed a crooked finger at the lump of the slacks.

"This?" The sheriff fingered the material thoughtfully.

"Yes, sir. I seen it and so I stops the cat and I climbs down to have me a better look. Didn't rightly know what the hell it was when I first seen it."

"So you found out it was somebody's pants."

"Yes, sir. Well, hell, there's all the time stuff layin' 'round the old gin, sometimes blowin' across the section, you know ..." He grinned self-consciously. "Sometimes I reckon them people drive out there nights forget some of their stuff."

"Yeah," the sheriff grunted.

"Well, sir, I picked up the stuff and seen it was them pants. I was thinkin', man, this must be a dame's stuff, somebody who sure left in a hurry, it bein' new and all. Then before I gets back on the cat, I see somethin' else, stickin' up out of the ground, close by the next post. It was one of them things." Again he leaned forward and this time he touched the shoe.

"This shoe?"

"Yes, sir. Well, hell, I starts walkin' along the post row and afore you knowed it, here's another shoe, up by the next post. After that I gets kinda curious, so's I keep walkin' along the row and each time I come to a post, there's one more of them things there."

"None of this was all together?"

"No, sir. Way I see it, I reckon whoever got rid of that there stuff, he starts plantin' the stuff separate-like, takes one of 'em, and digs a hole by the post and buries it out of sight."

"Why you reckon anybody'd do a thing like that?"

"Well, sir, if you don't mind my sayin' so, the man done that reckons as how no cat's gonna come close enough to go diggin' them things up, couldn't, not with them posts stand-in' like that."

The sheriff ran his tongue around the inside of his mouth, working to rid the taste of the long sleepless night from the backs of his teeth. "Then what'd you do?"

The farmer glanced at the silent preacher at his side. "Well, sir, I keeps on pickin' up stuff until there ain't no more. I even tried diggin' down by a couple of them posts after the last one, only there ain't no more stuff. I got all that the twister dug up." He lowered his eyes and his voice dropped. "I ain't smart, I reckon, only somethin' tells me there's somethin' right peculiar, me findin' all them clothes, newish clothes they is, too, buried down like that so's nothin' short of a tornado could uncover 'em, like it did." Again he looked at Joe Ben Potter and this time, as he continued, he did not take his eyes from the preacher. "I ain't much on church-goin' like some, I reckon, but right away I stands there lookin' at that mess of stuff I'm holdin' and somethin' tells me, this is somethin' Mr. Potter might be wantin' to know about." He brought his eyes to the sheriff and regarded him soberly. "So's I knock off workin' and gets my truck and carts this stuff over to the preacher. He says we gotta come see you and bring the stuff and so ..." He faltered helplessly and again began to roll the hat. "... that's what we done."

The sheriff glanced at the Reverend Joe Ben Potter. He eyed him thoughtfully, seeing the plain man, the dark, used suit, the sincere, honest eyes, the worried, pale lips. "You did right,

Mr. Potter, bringin' the stuff here." He hesitated. "It's hers, of course, you knew that."

Joe Ben Potter's eyes clouded. "Yes, Sheriff, I reckon as how I knew right off."

"And you know, if that's her stuff, she sure as hell ain't runnin' 'round the countryside stark naked as a buck ass goat."

Potter colored. "I reckon not."

"You're the boy's friend, aren't you?"

"I've known him since he was born," Joe Ben Potter said simply.

"You don't think he done it."

The preacher met the eyes of the sheriff levelly. "I'd stake my faith in my God he didn't," he stated quietly.

"My faith's kinda tied up in a lie detector down Austin that can't make up its mind, Reverend." The sheriff countered gently. "I don't know, it don't know." He turned his head and glanced across the room at the sleepy-eyed deputy slouched in the straight-backed chair tilted against the wall, his hat low over his brow. "Hey, Ray, you best get Bannock up and goin'. Get some of the boys together, too, shovels, spades and stuff. We got us some garden work to do."

"Just what is it you're plannin' to do, Sheriff?" Joe Ben Potter asked uneasily.

The sheriff turned mildly surprised eyes on the preacher. "Why, Reverend, we gotta go dig her up, don't we?"

From his window Harry Marvel watched the men coming out of the county jail building. There was the sheriff, a number of others carrying spades and shovels, and him, the big bastard, standin' out among them like a giant among pygmies. Harry's mouth moved convulsively and he reached up and took the dead cigar stub from his thick lips; he cleared his throat and spat on the floor close to his feet. He never took his eyes off them as they dispersed on the side-walk, some of them climbing into the large black sedan at the curb, the others going off down the street toward another big car. In a moment they had started the engines, the sounds of them seeping through the window.

Harry wasted no time. Breathless, excited, he crossed the room hurriedly, feeling in his trousers' pocket for his car keys. Whatever they was up to, this was something he wanted to see! He wanted to know what they were going to do with the bastard, where they were taking him now!

He hurried down the hall, clattered down the metal-edged wooden steps that led to the street and, once outside, he glanced at the cars. They were still there; the one nearest the far corner had just begun to back out slowly. He wasted no time. He cut into the alley and went to his car, jerking open the door, sliding under the wheel, got the car started and rolled down the alley.

As his car came poking out from the opening between the buildings, the first of the two county cars went by. The second car across the street backed out from its place, swung around to fall in line. Harry waited. His red-tufted fingers gripped the wheel until the blood left the knuckles. He could feel the sweat of excitement prickling on his brow, wetting the armpits of his clean sport shirt. He waited until the second of the cars had reached the stop light at the corner, waited, then picked up with the light change. He took his foot off the brake and rolled out into the open and turned left to take his place in the procession.

Harry Marvel was no fool. He kept a discreet distance behind the second car. They went out the broad street until the cavalcade came to the college intersection. They followed the campus until they came to the turning at the traffic islands and the turn there was right, west. They joined the morning stream of traffic heading for the highway that led out of town.

In the car ahead of Harry Marvel's Troy Bannock sat between two strange men. He sat straight, Watching the way they were going, remembering the other time, the night he and Nancy had driven this way, that night a thousand million years back. In the first car as it moved along steadily, passing the white-fenced areas where the sheep and cows of the college agricultural department grazed, Joe Ben Potter sat between the sheriff and the farmer, Bob Ryan, and his eyes were closed. Only the faint movement of his lips betrayed the fact that he was not dozing on the long ride. The preacher was seeking, asking, with a fervor and a passion which he had never before in his life brought to his calling.

The three cars came to the railroad tracks, bumped across them and dropped down the slight incline to the road past the big houses and finally out into the open country and the broad highway that led to Hobbs and the west.

Harry Marvel hunched over his steering wheel and frowned at the back of the big sedan ahead. He fished in the pocket of his shirt for a cigar, got one, stripped it of the cellophane with his free hand, bit into the end and readied it. He shoved it over to the corner of his mouth and reached automatically for the dashboard lighter. He never took his eyes from the rear of the big machine ahead and the bobbing blond head framed dead center in the rear window.

They'd rolled along easily, well within the speed limit, for five, maybe six miles before they came to the wreckage of the old gin. It lay scattered and strewn over the acreage, peaked in the center like the sail of an ancient vessel, its timbers angled and splintered over the whole of the field. It was here that the car suddenly slowed down and Harry Marvel saw the first of them turn off the highway and go bumping and rocking along the dirt road that led alongside the ruined building.

Harry scowled. If he were to follow right behind them, draw alongside them, there might be trouble again. Yet he had to know what was up, what they were doing with the big bastard, taking him joy-riding all over the county like he was the Duke of Edinburgh or something! He let the car slow itself, let the distance between him and the car ahead lengthen. Confusion was high in him; he couldn't go poking around where that goddam sheriff was, yet he had to know! The second car was turning in on the dirt road now, following the leader, swaying and lurching over the ruts of the field, veering out into the uneven ground to avoid the rubble. As he dropped the car speed to virtually a crawl, Harry saw that the first car had pulled up close to the post line bordering the newly-plowed field beyond, had stopped and that the men with their spades and shovels were climbing out, clustering around the hood of the car, waiting for the others to join them.

Harry Marvel drove on past the turn-off. He went on up the highway, creeping at a snail's pace, trying to pick up something in the rear-view mirror, something of what they were doing now, what they were up to. He could see nothing. Sonofabitch! he raged, why them shovels and all them men and them takin' that big goddam bastard out joy ridin' when he ought to be locked up tighter'n a tick behind them bars, stinkin' himself to death with bein' sorry for what he done!

He went a mile or so down the road and then he pulled over on the shoulder and sat there, the car engine idling, as he puffed nervously—quick, short, unsatisfying puffs—on the cigar wondering what the hell to do next.

"You stick to me close, boy," the sheriff ordered gruffly. "Wouldn't do a helluva lot of good you tryin' anything in this God-forsaken field anyway, I reckon." He turned to the farmer, Bob Ryan. "Now where's these damn posts where the stuff was buried?"

"Right down there." The farmer pointed some fifty yards away. He started walking, the sheriff and Troy following, with Joe Ben Potter close behind, and the men with their shovels and spades bringing up the rear.

When they had come to the first of the posts, the farmer stopped and pointed. "Here's where the pants were." There was only a slight indentation on the hard-packed ground, no indication that anything had ever been buried there. He moved on, went to the next post. "The shoe was here." There was some spilled dirt around a slight hole where the farmer had jerked the shoe free. And so it went, down along the post row, with the farmer pointing out each place, some shallow little hollows that showed where he had finished the tornado's job of unearthing the clothing.

When Bob Ryan had finished showing the sheriff and his men the short trail of his discovery, the party stopped. The sheriff glanced covertly at Troy. He stood impassively, his face masked, only the suffering of the past few days plain in his clear eyes.

"I don't reckon you want to say anything," the sheriff ventured. "Maybe like tellin' us where she is, save us the bother of pokin' around?"

The shadow passed over Troy's face. "I don't know nothin' about it," he said low.

"No," the sheriff grunted. "Didn't reckon you would." He turned to his men. "Well, boys, looks like we gotta do it on our own. Couple of you start over by the first post, others scatter out. Keep your eyes peeled for soft ground. When you think you got somethin', start diggin'." His glance shifted to Troy. "You don't try nothin' now, son. You stick close to your friend here, Mr. Potter. I got me things to do."

The men started working along the post line. They worked tirelessly, steadily, absorbed. None of them heard the bumping of the car as it edged around the wreck of the old gin; none of them saw Harry Marvel as he stepped out of the car, eased the door shut quietly and came to stand in the shadow of the saillike ruin, watching them sharply, the cigar clamped tight in the corner of his mouth.

Harry Marvel had sat there on the side of the highway, staring ahead, his eyes gone blank on the cars that came and went past him. He left off puffing the cigar, let it go dead in the corner of his mouth. He sat blinking, trying desperately to remember something, something he couldn't quite grasp, some vague, insistent something that demanded entry into his fogged brain. His hands suddenly remembered the feel of her, the softness of Rita's skin, the way her throat arched when she looked up at him.

As he came back near the road leading past the destroyed gin, he could see them working, strung out along the post line that bordered the plowed field, spading up the earth, digging a trench or something along the edge of the section. He drove down the cut-off, alongside the gin, to get a better look. He stopped the car and got out, shutting the door quietly. Standing in the shadow, he watched them, never taking his hard little eyes from the work they were doing.

"Didn't reckon on seein' you 'round so quick, Harry," the sheriff spoke suddenly. "I didn't reckon as how it'd be you at all. Seen the car come up but reckoned as how maybe it was somebody pokin' 'round the gin, maybe lookin' for somethin' they lost here one night."

"I am lookin' for somethin'," Harry Marvel said hastily.

"Yeah?" The sheriff had his eyes on the ugly stub of the cigar. "Reckon maybe you got a stake in what's goin' on at that. Reckon you'd like to come over and lend a hand? We're kinda short-handed, sure appreciate it."

"Reckon I'll just watch," Harry muttered.

"Come on along, Harry." The sheriff put his hand under Harry Marvel's elbow and nudged him gently, firmly. "Friend of yours over here you ain't seen in some days now. Maybe you got two friends over here, who knows?"

Harry swallowed and rolled the cigar nervously with the tip of his tongue. Christ Almighty, what ever made him come pokin' 'round in the first place! He hadn't seen the sheriff hangin' 'round the gin, clean forgot about him!

Harry found himself moving out of the shadow of the wrecked gin; he moved just ahead of the sheriff, powerless to resist the gentle, persuasive pressure beneath his arm.

As they came up to the first of the men digging along the post row, the sheriff's voice came low in Harry's ear. "Found poor Rita's clothes, all buried up close to the posts here, like somebody didn't want 'em turned up right soon." He gestured back toward the pile of the old gin. "Only little blow we had last night kinda screwed up somebody's plans."

They passed close to where Troy and Joe Ben Potter stood. Troy's face darkened and his fists balled into knots. He made a step forward, but the preacher's hand caught him, held him pinned in place. The sheriff and Harry Marvel stopped farther down the line. They stood watching, neither of them saying any-thing. The sheriff glanced again at the dried, dead cigar end in the corner of those ugly lips. He kept his eyes on Harry Marvel's face. There was something funny about the way the man kept watching the others dig, something that trapped the sheriff's wits, held him transfixed, unable to take his eyes away.

Harry was staring at the bite of the shovels in the earth. There was something about the way the blades cut cleanly into the ground, sank down so easily, then turned and came back with the rich earth spilling out over the hard ground. He stood staring, his cold little eyes wide; he wet his lips and the sweat beaded his forehead, glistening under the few reddish strands on his scalp.

Then terror spumed within him, without warning, without Harry being aware of where it had sprung from or why, or what had sparked it into sudden, strangling being. Terror rode the high seat within him. All he could see was the blade sinking down into the earth like that, a greedy, devouring thing, knifing down, biting, slashing, severing, eating hungrily into the soil. Harry Marvel ran his big hand over his sweat-streaked scalp. The thing inside him swelled, festered with each chuffing thrust. Suddenly there came a blinding, spewing blackening inside him as the thing burst. Wrenching from the sheriff's hold he plunged forward, snatched at the arm of the digging man; he spun him off balance and tore the shovel brutally from his hands.

"Not there, my God, not there, you'll cut her," he screamed. "Jesus Christ in Heaven, you'll cut her to bits doin' like you're doin'!"

As sudden as the thing had happened, it was done. Harry Marvel stood alone, apart, the shovel clutched in his big hands, the tears streaming down his fleshy, splotched cheeks, his breath labored and hoarse in the terrible silence that had come over the wreckage-strewn field.

It was the sheriff who finally spoke, who finally broke the paralysis of horror that gripped them. He spoke quietly, very quietly, not moving from the spot where Harry Marvel had left him.

"All right, Harry," he said tonelessly, "supposin' you dig for a while."

In the car, on the way back to town, the sheriff frowned. He rested his hands, palms down, on his legs and studied the moons of his nails. "Tell me somethin', Harry," he said to the broken figure at his side, "why'd you strip her after you strangled her, why that, too?"

Harry Marvel closed his eyes and forced down the sobbing. "I wanted her once more like before, all mine, all beautiful, all mine. She was all I had besides the rink, and she let all the others see. I just wanted to see her once more, beautiful like she was, and all mine."

# CHAPTER EIGHTEEN

Will Bannock sat in his favorite place on the porch and looked out over the seeding fields. In his heart there was peace and contentment now that had not found a welcome within him for many years. All the fear had come and gone away; now there was only the peace. He did not hear Cressy as she came to the door behind him, did not know she was looking down on him with eyes of warm affection.

"Pa?"

He raised his head but did not turn to look at her. "Yeah?"

"You all right?"

He nodded and stretched out his hand and she came and took it. "Yeah," he said softly. "I'm all right now." He looked up at her. "You're a good woman, Cressy, I'm right proud Tom's got you."

She nodded and smiled. "I'm proud, too, Pa."

He looked away, still holding her hand. "Bess all right?"

"She's lyin' down, just takin' a nap."

"Good. Tom?"

"Putterin' around the barn somewheres."

"Good man. Mind you take right good care of him."

He listened to her footsteps as she went back through the house. He drew a deep breath. He wished Joe Ben Potter was back from his honeymoon, would come see him, just visit for a spell.

His attention was caught by the sound of the approaching car. He watched as Troy wheeled in off the highway and came speeding down the road, smoking the whole of the front yard with the tawny dust. Troy brought the car skillfully around to stop by the front steps. Will could see the girl Nancy with him. They got out of the car at the same time, one on each side, and they met at the head of the walk and came arm-in-arm to the porch, Troy tall and straight and Nancy small and dainty and trusting, laughing up at him with all the flame and jewelry of youth.

When they reached the porch steps, they slowed their pace and it was she who spoke first. "Hello, Mr. Bannock."

"Hello, Nancy."

"Pa?" Troy's approach was shy almost; he stood apart from her, looking down on his father with soft eyes, backed by the strength of his ripened manhood.

"Yes, son?"

"Pa, there's somethin' I been wantin' to say."

"You ain't never had no trouble speakin' out before," Will observed dryly.

"It's about goin' to Austin and school," Troy faltered.

"Only a couple more months now," Will commented regretfully.

"I ain't goin', Pa," Troy blurted. "Me and Nancy's been talkin' things over. Pa, I'd like to stay on the place, go on workin' the land, after me and Nancy's married."

The great flood came washing up through Will Bannock, bringing strength to his arms, his legs, his back, and he looked up through suddenly stinging eyes at his son, his youngest, the one that could have been him all over again. "You ain't askin', son?" he offered softly.

Troy looked down at Nancy and brought her close to his side, held her firm and near within the circle of his big arm. "Not askin', Pa. I reckon somehow you knowed all along." He straightened slowly and his eyes went out over the wide stretch of the fields, far out to where the afternoon thunderheads had begun to bank once again along the unseen line. "There ain't nothin' in Austin I want no more," he said firmly, "I reckon as how a man can find all he wants right here at home."